Rule Your Own Fate . . .

While Tim is cooking the steaks, you see Peter, one of the guys you work with at the club. You have never really talked to him; he always seems to be surrounded by girls. Now he is walking directly toward you. You can feel your heart speed up.

"Well, hello there," Peter says to you. "This fire seems to be dying. Come on. Let's go find some firewood and get this thing roaring." He holds out his hand to help you up.

You look up at his tan face, his streaked hair, his strong, square jaw. *He looks more gorgeous than ever before,* you think. Then you remember that Tim is over at the barbecue cooking you dinner. You can't just walk off with Peter; Tim is such a sweetheart. But when you look at Peter, nothing else seems to matter. Besides, it's only to get some firewood.

If you go with Peter, turn to page 112.

If you wait for Tim, turn to page 114.

LET YOUR HEART CHOOSE!

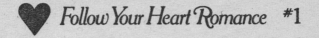 *Follow Your Heart Romance* #1

Summer In The Sun

Jan Gelman

AN ARCHWAY PAPERBACK
Published by POCKET BOOKS • NEW YORK

AN ARCHWAY PAPERBACK *Original*

An Archway Paperback published by
POCKET BOOKS, a division of Simon & Schuster, Inc.
1230 Avenue of the Americas, New York, N.Y. 10020

ISBN: 0-671-52444-5

First Archway Paperback printing February, 1983

10 9 8 7 6 5 4 3

AN ARCHWAY PAPERBACK and colophon are
trademarks of Simon & Schuster, Inc.

FOLLOW YOUR HEART is a trademark
of Simon & Schuster, Inc.

Printed in the U.S.A.

IL 5+

For Deborah, Lesley,
Domini, Laurie,
and Lisa

Read This First!

Summer in the Sun is not an ordinary romance book. It will not make sense if you try to read the pages consecutively. Instead, read until you come to a choice. Then follow your choice to the page indicated. Again, read until you come to a choice; then follow the instructions.

When you reach an ending, the book is not over. Just go back to the beginning and make different choices. You can lose—but only temporarily. If you've really messed up, don't worry. There is always another chance.

So follow your heart, read your way to romance, and have a good time.

You and your family have just moved to Los Angeles, home of the stars and the surfers. You, of course, know none of them. In fact, you don't know anyone and are not sure you want to. It seems as if every teenager you see is tan and beautiful. You are certain that everyone can tell from looking at you that you are an outsider.

Your parents keep telling you to go out and meet people. They seem to think it is such a simple thing to do. It wouldn't be so bad if school were in session; then you'd at least know some people in your classes. But it is the end of June and you are dreading the summer.

The only good thing about being in Los Angeles is the fact that you have the use of your uncle's car for the summer. At least you don't have to sit around the house all day long.

After a week of aimlessly driving around, feeling sorry for yourself, you decide that the only way to cope with no friends and nothing to do is to get a job. You spend the next week reading the ads and going for interviews. Finally you narrow your choices down to two.

If you choose to work at a hot dog stand on the beach, turn to page 2.

If you choose to be the children's counselor at an exclusive country club, turn to page 4.

You are already up when the alarm goes off at seven. In fact, you have been up since six, fussing with your hair; putting on eyeliner, taking it off; putting on lipstick, taking it off; putting on shadow, a touch of rouge. Finally you decide that working at a hot dog stand doesn't require any makeup at all, and you take it all off.

You go into the kitchen and start to make yourself a big breakfast of sausages, scrambled eggs, melon from California. *At least the state is good for something,* you think. As you are melting the butter for your eggs, you realize that your stomach feels queasy and you put everything away. You hear someone coming down the stairs and decide that you really don't feel like talking to anyone right now so you grab a peach and head out the door.

You are more than an hour early when you pull into the parking lot behind the hot dog stand. You are amazed to find the lot nearly filled. You squeeze your Honda between two battered VW bugs and look around. Every car has black rubber strips flapping from the roof, hanging down, sticking up, lying flat. You realize that they must be used to strap something down. But what?

The mystery is solved when you step out of the car and look down at the beach. The scene looks like a space movie about aliens. The sand is filled with blond-haired beings wearing rubber wet suits and carrying surfboards in their arms. There are even more surfers floating on their surfboards in the water, looking out at the ocean, waiting for the right

(continued on page 3)

wave. Every once in a while, they all ri
boards. Most of them fall; a few reach the sh
water upright.

While you are absolutely fascinated by the scene,
you are also completely intimidated. You sneak
back into your car, hoping no one has seen you.
After a few minutes someone walks into the lot,
straps his board to the car and begins to remove his
wet suit. You are not sure if he has a bathing suit on
underneath, and you do not want to find out. You
close your eyes and slip down in your seat, hoping
that he hasn't noticed you.

You are frightened as you huddle below the win-
dow—it is all so different from anything you have
ever known. Suddenly you are swept with a feeling
of panic. *I don't belong here*, you think. *It's a
different world and I don't fit.*

---

*If you would like to change your job choice
and work at the country club, this is your
last chance. Turn to page 4.*

*If the idea of being surrounded by surfers
intrigues you more than it frightens you, stay
with the beach job and turn to page 7.*

When you drive up to the entrance of the club for your first day of work, you are stopped at the gate-booth by the security guard. "Hi," he says. "May I help you?"

"I'm the children's counselor," you announce.

"Oh, yes," says the man. "They told me you were starting today. I'm Carlos. You have to park your car in the lot behind the arts-and-crafts cabin. Then you are supposed to report to Mr. Taylor in the main office. Good luck. Don't be nervous."

"Thanks," you say, wondering if he could tell from looking at you that you are scared stiff. You have never had a real job before.

Mr. Taylor is the man who interviewed you for the job. During your full half-hour interview, he never once smiled. He just asked you questions and took notes and ended by saying that he would review the notes. You had little hope when you left and you were amazed when he called three days later and offered you the position. *Probably no one else applied,* you think as you walk into his office.

A petite brown-haired women greets you. "Hi," she says. "You are the new counselor?"

You nod and introduce yourself. She tells you to have a seat; then she fumbles through her desk and takes out some papers. "These are some rules I typed up for you. Read them and sign at the bottom. Mr. Taylor will be back in a minute."

You take the papers and read:

(continued on page 5)

Arts-and-crafts sessions will be conducted from 9:00 to 12:00, not before 9:00 and not after 12:00.

The children will be with their parents from 12:00 to 1:00 and the cabin door will be locked.

You will be allowed to eat lunch from 12:00 to 1:00. The staff must eat in the kitchen, never in the guests' dining room.

Sports and games will begin at 1:00 and continue until 3:00.

Any spare time must be dedicated to helping the other staff members.

The staff is not to fraternize with the members nor use their tennis courts, swimming pool, bathrooms or locker rooms.

As you finish reading the rules, Mr. Taylor enters the room. He hands you two red T-shirts with the words *Silverwood Country Club Staff* written across the front in thin black type.

"Whenever you are working, you are to wear this shirt. Here are the keys to the crafts cabin and the supply room. I assume you have read the rules carefully. Do not try to interpret them, just follow them. If you don't have any questions, why don't you go start preparing for today's activities."

(continued on page 6)

Friendly, you think. *I wonder if he woke up on the wrong side of the bed or if he is always this way.* You smile sweetly and say, "Thank you. I will go down right now."

As you are on your way to the crafts cabin, Carlos, the security guard, calls to you. You walk over to the gate-booth. "How did you like the rules? They do not let us forget that we are staff," he says.

"I know what you mean. Is Mr. Taylor always that serious?" you say.

"Oh, yes. You will get used to him. The rest of the staff is great. You will meet them soon. I am sure you will have a good summer. Do not worry."

"Thanks," you say and then you walk over to the cabin. You open the door to a room about the size of a classroom. There are three picnic tables in the middle, covered with paint drops and glue stains. You are happy that you arrived early. You will have time to look through the supplies and decide what projects you will set up for the day. As you are looking through a box of beads, you hear a voice.

"What are we going to do today?"

Standing at the door are two boys and a girl, all about seven or eight years old. They are twenty minutes early.

If you get rid of them, turn to page 21.

If you decide to take them on, ready or not, turn to page 94.

You spend the next hour trying to be invisible. At nine o'clock you knock on the door of the hot dog stand.

"Hey," says John, the man who hired you. "How ya doin'?"

"Okay," you say. "Just a little nervous. I'm not sure if I can remember a thing you showed me." You try to remember how to turn on the grill, how to pull up the awnings, how to make the orange drink, how to set up the food. Everything is a big blur.

"Nothing to worry about," says John. "Cathy will be here in a minute. She's an old-timer—been working for two weeks already. I gotta be off. Have a good day."

You move to the counter at the front of the stand and look out at the beach. The surfers are gradually leaving, strapping their boards to the tops of their cars and driving off. The day people are arriving, spreading their towels, oiling their bodies. You cross your fingers in hopes that no one comes over to buy anything, and you look away whenever anyone looks in your direction.

You watch as a thin, pretty, dark-haired girl, wearing shorts and a bikini top, walks across the sand toward you. Her curly hair blows in the ocean breeze as she bounces along, greeting the surfers along the way. You can't quite believe how many guys she knows and you wonder if all California girls are like her.

After she has greeted nearly every surfer on the

(continued on page 8)

beach, the girl starts to walk toward the hot dog stand, still smiling.

"Hi," she calls from fifteen yards away. "I'm Cathy."

Immediately your stomach drops. What do you say to someone who bobs along the beach like that, talking to surfers?

When Cathy gets inside, it is obvious that she knows her job. Together you set up the grill, pile up the hot dogs and hamburgers, make the drinks and fill the popcorn machine. Cathy chatters the whole time about how much you are going to love California, about how she is going to introduce you to her friends and mostly about how many cute guys there are on the beach. She describes parties and barbecues and swimming in people's backyard pools. The more she talks, the more nervous you get. You cannot imagine ever being a part of all that.

As you listen and work, you observe the growing population on the sand. There are mostly teenagers sitting in groups. A family here and there. A few others in pairs or singles. You can't help looking at the cute guys as they walk by. But when you catch an eye and get a smile, you turn away, embarrassed.

As the morning moves on and business picks up, you find that your roving eyes keep returning to the good-looking lifeguard who is stationed between the stand and the water. He looks like every movie lifeguard you have ever seen—tall and broad-shouldered with a tan that looks as if it was painted on.

(continued on page 9)

His thick blond hair falls casually just below his ears. You cannot see his eyes but you know that they are blue.

"Hey, what are you thinking about?" Cathy asks.

"Oh, nothing," you say.

"Well," says Cathy. "Nothing's name is Jeff. And every girl on the beach is in love with him. Join the crowd."

You laugh, pleased to be part of a crowd. Two minutes later, while you are staring at Jeff and slicing tomatoes at the same time, the knife slips and you slash your finger. You can feel the pain pulsing through your hand as blood spurts from the cut. You stick your finger in your mouth to avoid a mess and try to act as if nothing has happened.

Then you remember that you have some Band-Aids in your purse. You are about to get one when Cathy sees the blood.

"Oh, wow," she says. "You better run down to the lifeguard and have him fix that up." She pauses. "Hmm. Maybe you're not as innocent as I thought."

If you would rather meet Jeff under other circumstances, turn to page 12.

If you rush off for professional first aid, turn to page 18.

"Okay," you say. "I'm ready. Let's go."

"Forward march," says Tony, and he blows the red whistle hanging from his neck.

You follow Tony to the kitchen where you get a hamburger, French fries and a Coke. Bobby is sitting alone at a table, so the two of you join him.

"Hi," says Bobby, his red baseball cap still on his head. He pushes the ketchup and salt out of the way, so that you can put your tray down, and he spills his 7-Up. It trickles down your bare legs.

"I'm so sorry," he says as you jump up.

"It's okay," you say.

"Don't let pretty girls get to you like that," Tony says, laughing. Bobby turns bright red.

A few minutes later, Peter enters. "Sorry I'm so late," he says. "Mr. Taylor and I had a bit of a tiff. I won't bore you with the details. But guess what? I finally got his okay for All Kids' Day. We can start planning it."

"All Kids' Day?" you ask.

"It's going to be four weeks from Monday," Tony says. "Since the club is usually closed on Mondays, we got Taylor to agree to let the recreation staff take over the whole place. No parents. No bosses. Only us and the kids. We're going to run games and activities all day long. You don't have to work if you don't want to, but we'd love to have you there. We need all the help we can get."

"We're having a meeting tomorrow at four-thirty to start planning," Peter says, interrupting.

"That sounds great," you say. "I'd love to do it."

(continued on page 11)

You all begin to throw out ideas for various activities. Before lunch is over you have come up with a watermelon-eating contest, an egg toss, and a million different kinds of races.

As you are walking out of the kitchen, Bobby slips you a napkin and whispers, "Read it."

"Do you want a ride back to your cabin in my cart?" you read.

You nod and smile at him. *How cute,* you think. When you reach the bottom of the stairs, Tony grabs your arm.

"I'll race you back!" he says.

You have just told Bobby that he could give you a ride back. When you look at him eating his ice cream, he reminds you of your little brother. Tony, on the other hand, reminds you of a rock star: a little crazy and a lot wonderful.

If you race Tony back, turn to page 24.

If you take the ride with Bobby, turn to page 69.

"I have some Band-Aids in my purse," you say. "I'll just use those."

"Oh, come on, this is your big chance."

"I'd feel really dumb; it's only a cut."

"To each his own," says Cathy. "Maybe I'll cut my finger and run down." She laughs.

You patch up your finger and then serve a woman an orange drink and a bag of potato chips. A large man orders a chocolate milk and three hamburgers. You wonder if he is going to eat them all himself.

As you wait on customers, you also get a chance to watch the beach. The surfers are gone and most of the action now is around the volleyball courts.

Earlier you noticed the volleyball nets in the sand—all up and down the beach. Now they are in action. Teams of two against two are running around on the courts, while groups of teenagers are standing and sitting on the periphery, watching, flirting, cheering the players and waiting for their turns to play.

You watch while a girl in a black and gold one-piece bathing suit is carried down to the water by two guys. She laughs and screams and wriggles as they toss her into the water. She comes back soaking wet, sneaks up behind one of the guys and pours sand all over him. Then she races down the beach giggling and looking over her shoulder. She is quickly pursued by the victim of her sand attack and once again is carted off to the water. You

(continued on page 13)

wonder if you will ever be thrown in the water or chased down the beach.

Your daydreaming is suddenly interrupted by the fluttering of wings in your face. You let out a scream. Startled, Cathy drops a bag of popcorn all over the floor and the small black bird begins to eat the spilled popcorn.

"This bird comes around almost every day," says Cathy. "She loves popcorn. The first time I saw her she scared me to death too. I call her B.F."

"What does it stand for?" you ask.

"Bigfoot. Look at her feet. One is bigger than the other. Okay, B.F., time to go. Come on, scram," says Cathy. The bird flies away. "We've got to get this mess cleaned up. Then we have to get some more ice cream out of the big freezer. It's hot already. We'll probably be real busy today."

You and Cathy work well together. For part of the day you are the cook and supply chief, while Cathy takes care of the orders, drinks, popcorn and ice cream. After a while, you switch. Before you know it, you are getting ready to go home.

Cathy puts the money in the safe and you count the cups. You can tell how many drinks have been sold by the number of cups that are missing. Together you close and lock the awning.

The next morning runs smoothly. As you work, you and Cathy chatter away about school, the

(continued on page 14)

beach, life in L.A. But mostly you discuss guys. Cathy can't stop talking about Mark, the love of her life. She asks if you would like to go out with his friend some day next week. Naturally, you say yes.

As you are washing off the counter around noon, you hear a little voice asking for ice cream. You glance around and don't see anyone. Then a hand appears on the counter. You look over and see a freckle-faced, redheaded boy in a baseball cap."

"Hi there," you say, leaning over the counter. "Are you all by yourself?"

"Yep," he answers.

You look along the beach for a stray mother or father, but there isn't any. You do notice, however, that Jeff the lifeguard is walking along the beach on his break. His fill-in, Steve, is standing by the station. Steve is nice; he came up yesterday and introduced himself. But he is at least thirty and definitely out of flirting range.

You turn your attention back to the little boy.

"I don't see anyone around that could belong to him," you say to Cathy and then you walk around to the outside of the stand and sit him up on the counter.

"How old are you?" asks Cathy from the inside.

"This many," he says, and he holds up three fingers.

"Where's your mommy?" you ask.

"Lost," he says, not at all concerned. "Can I have some ice cream?"

(continued on page 15)

"What's your name?"

"Billy," he answers. "Could I *please* have some ice cream?"

"Put it on my bill," you say to Cathy as she hands him a chocolate pop. "What do we do with lost kids?"

"I could be your helper," says Billy.

"I suspect your mom might be looking for you," you say.

"I've never had a lost kid before," says Cathy, "but my guess is that you're going to have to take him to the lifeguard—and there's no way out this time."

You look at Steve, then at Jeff disappearing down the beach. You know that Jeff will be back in a few minutes.

If you decide that you'd better bring Billy down now because his mother is probably worried, turn to page 28.

If you decide that Billy is happy enough eating his ice cream and that you are going to wait for Jeff to get back, turn to page 31.

"I'll be right back," you say to Mrs. Powell and you walk into the other room where Tom is putting his guitar away.

"I'd be glad to take you home," he says when you explain the situation.

You inform Mrs. Powell that you don't need a ride, and you walk outside with Tom to his red convertible bug.

"I wanted to talk to you anyway," he says. "I was wondering—well, we really played well together. What would you think about playing at a party with me next Saturday night? It's an adult party on a yacht, and they want some lively music. We could do some Beatles and some pop," he says.

"That's the stuff I love to play," you say. "But I'd better check with my parents." *Hmm,* you think, looking at his full handsome face. *Not only is he a fabulous musician, he's fabulous-looking, too. And that voice!*

When you arrive home, you give your number to Tom and run into the house. Your parents think that playing at the party will be good experience for you.

The next day Tom gives you directions to the yacht. "Be there by eight," he says, "and wear something black. We're going to be a great team."

You spend all of your free time during the week practicing piano. You decide that you are going to wear your black cords, a pink shirt, your mom's black blazer and a black bow tie of your dad's.

(continued on page 17)

At seven o'clock Saturday night, you are ready to go. You walk to your car and try to start it. Nothing. You try again. Nothing. There is not even a noise.

You run into the house and try to telephone Tom. No one is home at his house. Your dad has taken your brother to a movie, and your mother won't be home for another twenty minutes. The yacht is at least forty-five minutes away.

If you call a cab this minute, you could get there on time. It would cost you $25 however, and you are only making $35 for the whole night.

If you play it safe and call a cab, turn to page 105.

If you wait for your mother to get home, turn to page 109.

"Be right back," you say as you take a deep breath and head down to the lifeguard station. Your stomach is flipping. *Will he know I'm nervous?* you wonder, trying to relax.

As you walk down, you go over in your mind what you are going to say. *Hi, I work up at the stand and I cut myself. . . . No, that sounds dumb.* Before you figure out what to say, you are there.

"Hi. How are you today?" says Jeff. *Blue eyes,* you think. *I knew it.*

Trying to stay calm, you say, "Not too well. I mean . . . okay, but I kind of cut my finger."

"Let me have a look," he says, smiling at you. *Dimples too.*

He takes your hand and you feel your face flush.

"Oh, that's not so bad. I'll have you fixed up in a minute. So where have you been all of my life?" he says as he takes out his first-aid kit.

Not quite sure if he is being serious, you smile. "I just moved here and I'm working at the hot dog stand," you say.

"I know. I noticed you up there all morning. How do you like your job?"

"It's hard work, but it's fun," you answer. "It's my first job ever."

"By the way, I'm Jeff," he says, giving you a smile that almost knocks you off your feet. You love the way his eyes crinkle when he smiles.

As he takes your hand, you wonder if he can feel it shaking. *Why can't I be cool like Cathy?* you think.

(continued on page 19)

"If this hurts, let me know," he says as he paints your cut with an antiseptic.

"Thanks. I really appreciate it," you say.

"Oh, it's nothing. All I want in return is your beautiful body," he says.

You gulp and pull your hand away. You know he is just handing you a line, but what are you supposed to say to that? No one has ever talked to you that way before.

"Hey, honey, I'm only joking. Don't be so uptight."

Honey? you think. *What a phony.* "I'm afraid my New York background never prepared me for California lifeguards," you say. You've read about people like him. They're full of baloney. But why, you wonder, is your heart pounding?

"Maybe we can get together some night?" he says, looking into your eyes.

I am definitely not ready for this guy, you think. *But those eyes, that body.* You have never been so close to someone like him before. He makes your head spin. You are trying to come up with something clever to say when a tall, beautiful redhead walks over and puts her arm around Jeff's shoulder.

"Hi, big boy," she says. "I just came down to ask you if you were going to the party tonight. But excuse me, I didn't realize that you were busy. Is that your little sister?"

You are crushed. *Who does this girl think she is? Why does she have to come along and embarrass me like this?*

(continued on page 20)

"No, it's not my sister, Karen. She works up at the stand. Oh, and yeah, I'll try to make it to the party. It sounds like fun."

"Great. I'll look for you there. Oh, by the way, honey," she says to you. "Just out of curiosity, how old *are* you?"

You could kill her. *She just wants Jeff to hate me,* you think. You are sure Jeff is at least twenty. You know that he will never bother with you if he knows you are only sixteen.

If you tell your real age, turn to page 30.

If you lie and say that you are nineteen, turn to page 34.

"Hi. I'm so glad you guys are early," you say. "I need your help. This is my first day and I want everybody to know I'm here. Will you be my announcers?"

"Sure," say the kids.

"Great. Tell all the kids that we're going to be having arts and crafts from nine to twelve and I can't wait to meet them."

The kids run off arguing about where they should go first, and you continue your investigation of the supply closet. You have just decided to make pompom monsters with movable eyes and felt feet, when you hear a male voice.

"Well . . . well . . . well."

You look up and see three guys standing in the doorway. They look like the Three Musketeers. Well, maybe a little closer to Three Mouseketeers. On the left is a tall blond in blue shorts and a red and white striped visor. In the middle is a wiry guy in jeans and a cowboy hat with sun-bleached blond streaks in his dark hair. On the right is a thin boy with a sandy head of hair that looks like a mop. Perched on top of the mop is a red baseball cap. They are all wearing red staff T-shirts.

"Well, hello," you say, startled.

All three march in and sit at a table. "What are we making today?" asks the blond.

"Hey," says the cowboy, "who cares what we're making? The important thing is that the new counselor is much prettier than we expected. Don't you agree, guys?"

(continued on page 22)

"Most definitely," says the blond.

"Since we know you and you don't know us, permit me to perform the introductions," says the cowboy. He gestures with his hat toward the blond. "This is Tony, our famous lifeguard. A rather pleasant fellow, but certainly not your type. And this"— he points to the mop-haired one—"is Bobby. He rides around on the driving range in a caged golf cart that magically collects balls as it rolls. He's sixteen. A trifle young, I would say. And then there is *moi,* Peter. I am in charge of all four of Silverwood's magnificent horses. I, of course, am just right."

"Can we make lanyards?" asks Tony. Before you can answer, he picks up a piece of yarn, ties it around Peter's neck, and holds the other end. "That's just to keep him away from you. Watch out for him. He's dangerous. Now then," adds Tony, "let's get to the important stuff. What time is your lunch?"

"From twelve to one," you say.

"Oh, Tony, what a pity. You have a swimming lesson at twelve," says Peter. "But, of course, I happen to be free. How would you like to dine with me, my dear?"

"Sure," you say. You are loving their act and Peter is definitely your first choice for lunch. There is something wonderfully incongruous about his blue jeans, his cowboy hat, and his smooth style. You look around and notice that the third Mouseketeer has disappeared.

(continued on page 23)

"I shall pick you up at noon," Peter says, as the two of them leave.

At twelve, you are wiping up the glue from the tables when Tony walks in.

"What did you make for me?" he says.

"Here you go," you say, throwing him a pompom with purple feet and wiggly eyes.

"Wow, that's neat," he says. "If you put a cowboy hat on its head, it would look just like Peter. You ready to go? My lesson was canceled."

"What about Peter?" you say, looking around.

"Oh, him? He got in trouble and has to clean up the barn," Tony says, laughing. "He sent his apologies."

If you believe Tony and you go to lunch with him, turn to page 10.

If you think Tony is putting you on and you want to wait for Peter, turn to page 115.

"You got it!" you say and race off toward the crafts cabin. Tony passes you in a second.

"Better luck next time," he says when you reach the cabin. Then he trots off to the pool, intentionally stumbling and tripping over his feet.

Clown, you think. "I demand a rematch," you yell. "You were just lucky." He laughs and keeps going.

Over the next few weeks, most of your free time is dedicated to preparing for All Kids' Day. Every day at lunch, a group of you meet; and after work, you usually go for pizza or burgers. Altogether there are eight of you in the planning.

As each day goes by, you are becoming more and more infatuated with Peter. Sometimes he seems so intense and controlled; other times, he reminds you of a French nobleman. You love his soft smile; and when he walks, he has such a strong, determined stride. The cowboy hat adds just the right touch.

But Peter seems to treat you like his kid sister. When you visit him at the barn, he gives you jobs to do—things like shoveling manure or brushing horses. Very romantic! You have never seen him with another girl, though, and you suspect that he is in love with his horses. He hardly ever goes out with the gang, and he frequently stays late doing stable chores. Mostly you see him during planning sessions.

You are eager for All Kids' Day to come. The preparations have given Bobby excuses to visit you ten times a day. At ten o'clock he arrives with an

(continued on page 25)

idea for some event. At eleven, he modifies his idea and presents a new one. Some of his "better" ideas have been: shaving-cream fights, a headstand tournament, and a peanut-butter eating contest. He is like a puppy dog—cute, lovable and always under your feet.

Tony has been getting on your nerves too. He can never be serious. And worse, whenever you are in the middle of a conversation with Peter, Tony seems to appear. He always has some wacky story or scheme. One day at lunch you told him that you were craving a chocolate bar. The next day he brought you a giant Hershey kiss, bigger than a baseball. He's fun to kid around with because he's such a nut; but your interest is purely on the level of "just friends."

Tony, on the other hand, wants to be more than friends. You know he has a crush on you. Fortunately, most of the time, you only see each other in a group situation. But one morning Tony comes by and asks you out to a movie.

You are sure you would have a good time with him. He's funny and he makes you laugh. But Peter and Tony are best friends and you know that Peter would never ask you out if you went out with Tony.

If you go to the movies with Tony, turn to page 79.

If you say no, turn to page 83.

You are sure that once the members hear the story they will insist that Carlos be rehired. It's true that he did break the rules, but there were extenuating circumstances and he should certainly be given another chance.

You, Peter, Tony and Bobby decide that you will each talk to the members that you know best and see if you can convince them to call a special board meeting that afternoon.

You talk to the parents when they bring their kids for the afternoon session. As the day progresses, you feel confident that the members will rectify Mr. Taylor's poor decision. Every person you talk to seems to agree with you, but then you remember it was one of the parents that complained.

Could it be that they are agreeing with me to my face and not really meaning it? you wonder.

"Honey, you're absolutely right," says Mrs. O'Brian, your favorite parent. "I'm behind you a hundred percent and I'm going to insist we have that meeting, but I'm afraid there are a lot of members here who won't agree with me."

Is it really possible that rules could be that rigid? you wonder. *Aren't human beings more important than rules?*

At five o'clock the board members file into one of the meeting rooms. You and your friends wait outside. The members are still in there at six.

"It's obviously not as simple as we see it," says Bobby.

(continued on page 27)

"It isn't a matter of simple and complex," says Peter. "It's a matter of values."

"They probably voted against us in the first five minutes," says Tony. "Now they're in there drinking, using up time, just to make it look as if it was a tough decision."

At six-fifteen the door opens. Mrs. O'Brian is the first one out. She walks over to you. "I tried and lost. They're afraid that if they hire Carlos back, they'd be setting a precedent. I'm sorry."

"So am I," you say. "I quit."

"Me too," say Tony, Bobby and Peter.

"Tell Taylor to put our checks in the mail," you add.

There are tears in your eyes as the three of you go to your separate cars and agree to meet at the pizza place. It isn't because of losing your job that the tears are streaming down your face. It's because you've learned something about people that you really don't want to know.

Thank goodness the people I care about are willing to stand up for what they believe, you think as you pull up in front of the pizza place and see your friends.

The End

You lift Billy off the counter and start toward the lifeguard. The sand is burning hot and you are both barefoot.

"Ouch," squeals Billy. "Pick me up."

As you run with Billy in your arms, you can feel the ice cream trickling down your arm. Steve greets you.

"Well, hello. What have you got there?"

"This is Billy and he's this many years old," you say, imitating your young friend.

By now Billy has managed to drip goo all over your shirt and down your neck. Steve puts a towel on the sand for Billy to stand on, and you try to wipe off the drips and drools.

"I'll call the beach patrol and have someone come get him. They'll find his parents. Thanks a lot for bringing him down."

"No problem," you say. "Listen, if you pick him up, watch out for the slobbers. See you later, kiddo."

When you get back to the stand, there is a rush of hot dog and hamburger orders. Then there follows a lull. You and Cathy are just beginning to relax when a male voice yells, "Heads up," and a volleyball misses your head by an inch. It crashes into the grill and knocks over a stack of raw hamburgers.

Seconds later, a tall, dark-haired guy with a headful of curls appears. "Do you happen to have an extra volleyball around?" he asks.

"Well," you say. "As a matter of fact . . ."

(continued on page 29)

"I'm really sorry," he says. *Those green eyes look great with his dark hair,* you think. "I can't believe that the ball came all the way over here." Then he notices the mound of hamburgers on the floor. "Oh brother. Listen, I'll pay you for the ruined hamburgers. I don't want you two to get in trouble. How much do I owe you?"

You look at the pile of meat. The six hamburgers on the bottom are ruined, but you wonder about the ones on top of the pile.

If you think that it is better to be safe than sorry and you decide to throw away all the fallen hamburgers, turn to page 41.

If you decide that you can save the ones on top, turn to page 35.

"Sixteen," you say, looking her straight in the eye. "Thanks," you say to Jeff. "I've got to get back to work."

You look at Karen, who is draped seductively against the lifeguard chair. "Bye, honey," she says. "Don't get lost."

You give her a dirty look. *Witch,* you think. You would love to bury her in the sand, three feet down.

When you get back, you tell Cathy what happened. To cheer you up, she tells you about a party at seven o'clock that night.

"It should be a good party; they're even serving dinner. Why don't you come with me? Jeff might be there. What do you say?"

You wonder if it is the same party Karen was talking about. As you are considering the invitation, you remember that you are supposed to take your brother to his Little League game at six o'clock. You won't be able to do both.

If you keep your promise to your brother, turn to page 37.

If you decide that your mother can take your brother to the game, turn to page 44.

As Billy drips chocolate ice cream all over himself and the counter, you watch for Jeff. *A few minutes won't matter that much,* you think.

"Hi," Billy says to a short, bald man who is buying a hot dog. "Don't you want some ice cream?"

"Of course I do, but not right now," the man responds, laughing.

"Can I have a bite?" he asks a girl who has just bought a hamburger.

"Sure," she says and gives him one.

"Don't buy a hot dog," he tells a woman. "They have poisons."

"Well, then," she says, "I'll have a taco."

You and Cathy are enjoying Billy's performance when you notice that Jeff has returned. "Be right back," you say to Cathy.

Cathy smiles. "Good luck!" she says.

"You want a piggyback ride?" you ask Billy, remembering how hot the sand is.

"Sure do," he says. "Ride 'em, cowboy!" You gallop to the lifeguard station.

"Yahoo!" Billy yells. "Look at me."

Jeff turns around. "Hey, cowboy, how's it going?" he says, smiling. He is even cuter up close than he is from a distance. His blue eyes crinkle when he smiles and he has dimples in his cheeks.

"Hi," you say. "I've got a lost kid here. Can you help me out?"

"I sure can. Come here, cowboy," Jeff says, walking behind you and lifting Billy off your shoul-

(continued on page 32)

ders. You feel shivery when he touches your shoulder. *Now what?* you think.

Jeff twirls Billy around and then sits him on the lifeguard chair. Billy is delighted.

"So, where did you find this little rascal?" says Jeff.

"He wandered up to the beach stand and wanted ice cream," you answer.

"And I can tell that you gave him some. It's all over him," he laughs.

"His mother is lost," you say.

"I'll call the beach patrol and they'll . . ."

Jeff's sentence is cut short as he dashes toward the water. He dives in and pulls a little girl from under a wave. Panting, he carries the hysterical girl to the station.

You hold her on your lap until she is calm. "You look like a drenched little mouse," you say as you bounce her on your knee.

"You're great with kids," Jeff says.

"Thanks," you say. "I love them."

"Listen, I know you have to get to work, but could I ask a big favor? The water is getting crowded and Steve is still on his break over by Station 17. Could you run down and tell him to get back here?"

"Sure," you say. "Can you handle these two troublemakers?"

"I'll try," he says.

You jog down and find Steve stretched out on a

(continued on page 33)

towel. When the two of you return, Jeff is being attacked by a Frisbee.

"Pow," Billy yells. The little girl laughs.

"Listen," you say. "Why don't I take the kids up to the stand with me and when the patrol gets here, send them up."

"That would be great," Jeff says. "I'll tell you what. I definitely owe you one! How about a bite to eat after work?"

"Great," you say, trying to hold in your scream.

You take the little girl's hand and put Billy on your back. As you walk back to the stand, you cannot feel Billy hitting you on the head. In fact, you cannot even feel the ground. You are walking on a cloud.

The End

You don't want to give Karen the satisfaction of knowing that you are sixteen.

"Nineteen," you say as you turn the other way, not wanting to look Jeff in the face while you lie. "Thanks for everything," you add. "I've got to get back to work." You hurry off up the beach.

Later that afternoon, as you are breaking up a mustard fight between two little boys, Jeff taps you on the shoulder.

"Hi, sweetheart. I was on my break and I decided to come say hello. We never did get to finish our conversation."

"Don't mind my mess," you say, scraping mustard off your arm. "I seem to have turned yellow."

"So, tell me," Jeff says, ignoring the mustard, "what do you do with yourself during the year?"

Where would I be if I were nineteen? you think.

"I'm going into my second year of college," you say, pleased that you were able to think so fast. "U.C.L.A."

"Really?" says Jeff. "You look younger than that. I thought you were making that stuff up about being nineteen just to get Karen off your back. My sister is at U.C.L.A. too. I'm a senior at Santa Monica High School."

You blew it.

The End

"The good news is that I think I can salvage the hamburgers on top," you say. "The bad news is $6 for the ones on the bottom."

He gives you the money, apologizes and goes back to his game. You place the top six hamburgers back on the pile and fill a little girl's order for three small Cokes, two corn dogs, and a frozen Milky Way.

Cathy is refilling the orange-drink dispenser when Jeff appears.

"Hi," he says. "You're new here. I'm Jeff. I'm the lifeguard."

"Oh," you say, as if you haven't been staring at him for two days. "Nice to meet you. Can I get you something to eat?"

"A hamburger and a Coke, please."

"Rare, medium or well-done?" you ask, wanting to give him deluxe service.

"Nobody's ever asked me that before," he says. "Medium is fine."

"Shall I grill the bun?" you ask, watching the line behind Jeff grow, but figuring he's worth the extra work.

"I can't wait to eat this hamburger," says Jeff. "This hot dog stand is really coming up in the world. Thanks."

"Well," says Cathy when Jeff leaves, "I didn't know we were grilling buns. That was pretty cool. Boy, is he cute! Listen, if he comes back for dessert, I want to wait on him."

(continued on page 36)

You reluctantly agree. Meanwhile, there are seven grumbling people standing in line. Before you finish with the first person, Jeff reappears.

"Be with you in a minute," Cathy calls, but Jeff walks to the front of the line and talks directly to you.

"Can I talk to you privately?" he asks. "Come around to the back door."

You look at the long line of people waiting to be served.

If you tell Jeff that you are too busy right now, turn to page 48.

If you rush back to meet Jeff, in spite of the crowd, turn to page 54.

You know that Jamie will be disappointed if you don't take him to the ball game. You and he have a very special relationship and it's based on the fact that you have never gone back on a promise. He, too, is having a hard time adjusting to a new life, new friends, new neighborhood. You're one of the few stable elements in his life and you cannot let him down.

You also are not so sure you would be comfortable in the scene Cathy has been describing. Big parties have never been your thing, and big parties where you don't know anyone have always scared you.

"Thanks," you say to Cathy's invitation. "But I promised Jamie I'd take him to his Little League game. Chauffeuring Jamie is one of the jobs that goes along with the car; I really can't get out of it."

"Well," says Cathy, "if you don't go where the guys are, you're not going to meet any."

"Is that all you do out here?" you ask. "I mean, is it really true that if I don't go to parties all the time, I'll never get asked out?"

"Hey, look. I'm me and you're you. I spend as little time with my family as I possibly can. We get along a lot better that way," says Cathy.

You are not sure where to go with this conversation. The fact is that you don't mind being with your family, especially your brother. Luckily, the rest of the afternoon is very busy and you finish up just in time to scoot home.

(continued on page 38)

Jamie is sitting on the front step when you pull up. His Tiger cap is backwards on his head and he looks so serious in his blue and white striped uniform that you have to hug him when he jumps in the car.

"Come on," he says. "I don't want to miss batting practice."

You are glad you kept your promise.

"We're going to whip the pants off the Aces," says Jamie. "They've got this tall skinny pitcher named Jerome who strikes everybody out, but there's no way he's going to get me. I am going to connect with that ball and smash it over the fence."

"Well, I'll be cheering for you, Jamie. I brought you a hot dog for extra energy. I made it special for you."

"Oh boy," says Jamie, eating the whole thing in three bites. "Those Aces don't know what's coming. We're gonna kill them."

When you arrive at the field, it is a half hour before game time. There are a few boys batting, some throwing the ball around the infield, others squirting each other with water guns on the sidelines. You climb up into the bleachers and lie down, relieved to be resting for the first time since nine A.M. It's been a long and exciting day. You close your eyes.

You are awakened 45 minutes later by cheering kids.

"I did it. I did it," screams Jamie as he crosses home plate. You doubt that he noticed the fact that

(continued on page 39)

you slept through his home run and you don't intend to tell him. He races toward you, screaming, "I did it. I did it."

"That rates an ice cream sundae after the game," you say.

"I knew I was going to get a home run off Jerome."

Unfortunately for the Tigers, Jamie's home run is the only team hit of the game. The final score is 12 to 1, Aces.

Jamie comes racing up to you when the game is over. "Okay, okay. Now let's get our ice cream."

"Can we join you?" says a male voice walking in your direction from the Aces' bleachers.

At first you don't recognize him in regular clothes.

"Jeff, the lifeguard from the beach," he says.

You cannot believe that he is standing there.

"What are you doing here?" you ask. "I thought you were going to a party."

"The truth is, I'm not much of a party person. I'd much rather take my brother Jerome to Little League. Well, what do you say? Since we all have something to celebrate, why don't we do it together? If this is your local Little League team, I'll bet we'll be going to the same high school too."

"High school? How old are you anyway?"

"Eighteen."

"You sure seem a lot older. I thought you were at least twenty."

"It's an act," says Jeff. "People expect a life-

(continued on page 40)

guard to be tough and macho and smooth. I play the part, but it's not what I'm like at all. I hope you'll let me show you what I'm really like."

"Oh, brother," says Jamie. "Come on, let's go get that ice cream and cut the mush."

"Yeah," says Jerome. "We played a tough game. Let's get the after-game show on the road." The boys run ahead.

Jeff looks down at you and he takes your hand. His blue eyes are softer, his smile warmer, his manner more gentle than his lifeguard personality. "Ten-year-olds don't know anything," he says, squeezing your hand.

The End

You look at the mound of hamburgers on the floor and decide that it really would not be safe to save any of them.

"I hate to break this to you, but that volleyball shot is going to cost you $12."

"Twelve bucks? That's a good enough reason to quit volleyball," he says, laughing, his brown curls bouncing. "Listen, is it okay if I pay you later? I don't have enough money in my pocket and my wallet is over by the court. Oh, and will you do me a favor? As long as I'm playing for the meat, I'd like to take it home. Would you stick it in a bag and keep it in your refrigerator for me?"

"Sure," you say, wondering what in the world he is planning to do with dirty meat.

At the end of the day, he returns to pay you and pick up his bag of hamburgers.

"By the way," he says as he is about to leave. "My name is Kevin, and I really am sorry I crashed your stand. Then again," he adds, smiling broadly, "maybe I'm not so sorry. It did give me an excuse to meet you."

As he talks, you notice his green eyes and his open smile. His curly dark hair gives him a different look from most of the guys on the beach. Actually, you're kind of glad it happened too. *Maybe something more will come of this*, you think. But then you think about his going off with all that dirty hamburger meat and you wonder if he might be a little weird.

(continued on page 42)

The next day, the beach is hot and crowded. By two in the afternoon, you and Cathy have sold two hundred drinks and the line seems endless; you are exhausted.

"I'm taking a twenty-minute break," you tell Cathy. "And when I come back, it's your turn."

"Sounds great," she says, "if I'm still alive in twenty minutes."

You are grungy and hot and all you want to do is sit somewhere and relax. As you are walking past the volleyball court in a semi-daze, someone taps you on the shoulder.

"Hi," says Kevin. "I just wanted to apologize again."

"Oh, don't worry about it," you say. "I feel bad that I had to make you pay so much."

"Hey, look, it was my fault. Listen, how would you like to hit a few with me?"

"Oh, no," you answer. "I would ruin the game."

"No, no," says Kevin. "I don't mean a game. I mean just hit some on the side. I have to warm up for my game."

You look at the crowd of kids sitting around the court. The oil on their bodies glitters in the sun as they lie around looking as though they were born on the beach. *Hit a few? With all these people watching?*

You have played volleyball twice in your life—and both of those times were in eighth-grade gym class. You can't even remember how to hold your

(continued on page 43)

hands when you hit the ball. And besides, you are on the verge of collapse.

On the other hand, that headful of curls and those emerald eyes are very appealing, and he might turn out to be an interesting teacher.

If you tell Kevin you are too tired to play, turn to page 47.

If you decide that you will not let pride and exhaustion stand in the way of a possible relationship, turn to page 50.

"Let me check with my mother and make sure she can drive Jamie to his game," you say, and you run off to the phone booth.

When you return with the good news, Cathy is running around madly. There are eight impatient people in line. You rush over and start taking orders. Cathy works the grill while you get the drinks, popcorn and ice cream. The two of you run around all afternoon as though you are part of a slapstick movie, but instead of getting smaller, the line grows. After a while, you and Cathy get silly and start to laugh. That's when the orders get all mixed up. People keep returning their hamburgers.

"It was supposed to have a tomato," says one.

"I specifically said no ketchup," says another.

"Where's my relish?" says a third.

You and Cathy can't stop laughing. When the siege is finally over, you have managed to get ketchup on your face, mustard on your arm and popcorn down your shirt. Cathy has relish all over her shirt and soda on her shorts. You both begin laughing again and do not stop for at least a half hour.

"Let's go to my house after we close," says Cathy. "I'll find you something to wear and we can go to the party together."

You follow Cathy to her house and park behind her on the street.

"How about some hot apple pie with ice cream?" she says as she pops a frozen pie into the microwave.

(continued on page 45)

"Great," you say. "But isn't the party for dinner?"

"Sure, but I always eat before I go to a dinner party," says Cathy. "That way I'm not hungry and the guys never find out what a pig I really am."

"I'm just the opposite," you say. "When I go to parties I eat, just to avoid talking to people I don't know. Sometimes I play the piano—that works too. I'm kind of nervous about this party. I won't know anyone."

"Don't worry," says Cathy. "You'll do fine."

As you eat your apple pie, you can feel your stomach tightening up. *Oh well,* you think, *a party where I don't know anyone is better than no party at all.*

When you are dressed, you and Cathy leave for the party.

It's open, says a sign on the front door. *Come on in.*

You walk into what is probably the most beautiful room you have ever seen. It is all white—the rugs, the chairs, the couches, the lamps. There is even a huge white grand piano at the far end of the room. The only color is in the paintings: they are swirls of yellow, spirals of blue and red, and vibrant, churning combinations of all three.

For a long time you just stand there, lost in the grandeur. When you finally come back to earth, you realize that the room is filled with strange faces, and Cathy has disappeared.

(continued on page 46)

Carefully you move your eyes from one group of people to the next, hoping to see Jeff, the lifeguard; but he isn't there. Then you notice *her,* Karen from the beach. "Is that your little sister?" she had asked Jeff in a tone of voice you thought was reserved for overacted movies. Terrific. You know one person at the party and she's a monster.

But you can't help watching her. There's a look in her eyes that seems to attract men . . . sort of like the bug lights that attract mosquitoes. She is surrounded by guys. You stand there staring, wondering how all those guys can fall for such a phony style. You watch her change positions every few minutes, sticking out her hip, twisting her torso, lowering her head and looking up with big eyes.

You have almost forgotten how uneasy you are when Cathy grabs your arm. "I can't believe you're still standing where I left you," she says. "Come on, I'll introduce you to some people."

"It's okay," you say. "I think I'd rather be background."

"Well, you can't just stand there all night. You might take root. Besides, it looks dumb. Hey, how about playing the piano? Come on," she says, pulling you into the room.

If you play, turn to page 49.

If you tell Cathy that you'd rather get something to eat in the next room, turn to page 53.

"I'd like to," you say, "but I'm really tired and I just have to sit for a few minutes."

"Oh, don't worry about it. Actually I don't need to warm up anyway. How about a game of backgammon?"

That's more like it, you think, knowing that you rarely lose in backgammon.

"Now that sounds great," you say.

You follow Kevin over to his towel and start setting up a board. A tall, broad-chested football-player type and a short, heavyset guy walk over and sit next to you.

"You better watch out," the taller one whispers. "Don't let Kevin hustle you. He's never been beat down here."

Kevin blushes and you laugh. The shorter one announces that he gets to play the winner and that he's rooting for you.

You can tell after five minutes that Kevin is a very good player. However, as the game goes on, it is clear that unless you make a stupid move, you are going to beat the champ of the beach and ruin his image. *Some guys are really touchy about losing to a girl,* you think.

If you decide that you will play your best game and not worry about Kevin's reputation, turn to page 63.

If you decide to let Kevin win and play it safe, turn to page 64.

Even though you are dying to know what Jeff wants, you can't keep the people waiting while you carry on your flirtation. You smile and raise your eyebrows seductively, the way they do in the movies. "I can't get away now," you say. "Can we meet a little later?" You picture yourself and Jeff holding hands and running together into the water.

"I have something very important to tell you," he says. "It won't wait. And I really don't want to say what I have to say in front of all these people."

Even though you feel irresponsible leaving the work to Cathy, there is an urgency to Jeff's tone and you realize that you have no choice.

Turn to page 54.

"Oh, okay. I'll give it a try," you say to Cathy.

As you sit down on the piano bench, you glance over your shoulder. Karen is still entertaining most of the men in the room. You hate her. Your stomach is doing flip-flops and you are not sure if your shaking hands will be able to play.

You begin with "Hey Jude," one of the many Beatles' songs that you know. As your fingers move across the familiar keys, you can feel yourself beginning to relax. Cathy starts to sing. Gradually, other voices join in. When you look over your shoulder, you notice that there is a crowd around you. You finish your first song and continue with "Birthday," another Beatles' song. This song is more lively and attracts even more people.

You are feeling terrific. You know that when you finish playing, people will come over and start talking to you. You turn around for a reassuring look at the crowd and see Karen. She is sitting in one of her seductive positions on the couch, but no one is paying attention. All the guys are standing around you.

The End

"Sure," you say, "I'd love to hit some, but I'm really bad."

Kevin puts his hand on your shoulder and looks down into your eyes. "Hey, don't worry about it, okay?" he says. Then he pauses, his green eyes smiling into yours. "I'll be happy to show you a few things."

Kevin picks up a volleyball. "Come on," he says, "let me see what you can do." He hits the ball to you. You return it in the wrong direction. He tries again. This time you hit it back over your head.

Kevin walks over and takes your hands. He puts them in the correct position and explains what you are doing wrong. His touch is gentle; his voice is soft. You love the way those dark curls frame his face.

Over and over Kevin hits with you and then offers instruction. He speaks with easy confidence, and you cannot believe his patience.

By the time your twenty minutes are up, you feel as though you have known him forever.

"You're a great teacher," you say.

"Uh-uh," says Kevin. "I have a great pupil." He walks you back to the stand. "How about another lesson tomorrow?"

"Sure," you say, "I'd love it."

When Cathy returns from her break, you are still floating. "Hey, space case, who are you dreaming about? Mr. Volleyball?" Cathy asks. "He's not too bad. A little weird about dirty hamburgers, but otherwise not too bad."

"Yeah," you say, barely hearing her.

(continued on page 51)

The next day, you see Kevin playing volleyball. But by three o'clock he still hasn't stopped by. At ten minutes before five, he finally appears.

"Hello, student," he says, smiling. "How are you today?"

"Great," you say.

Just then, a dog runs into the stand and grabs an ice cream out of your hand. You are startled and let out a screech.

"That dog belong to anyone here?" asks a man in a light green uniform.

"He's mine," says Kevin.

"Well, keep him on a leash," says the man.

Kevin agrees and the man leaves.

"Is that really your dog?" you ask.

"No," Kevin says, "but I didn't want this pup to be dragged off to the pound. They'll kill him if nobody claims him. I'll bring him down to the animal shelter. At the shelter we keep them whether they're claimed or not."

"We?" you ask.

"Oh. I work at the shelter part-time."

"So that explains it," you say.

"Explains what?" Kevin asks.

"You took home twelve dirty hamburgers the other day. I just couldn't figure it out."

Kevin laughs. "You must have thought I was pretty weird, huh? Listen," he says, "I better bring this dog to the shelter. I was wondering . . . well, if you would be interested in doing something Thursday night?"

(continued on page 52)

"Sure," you say, trying not to show your excitement.

"Great," he says. "I'll see you tomorrow."

You watch as he leads the dog into a dark blue Datsun.

Tomorrow comes and goes, but Kevin never shows up. All day Wednesday you keep looking for his blue car in the lot and his brown curly hair by the volleyball courts. You keep telling yourself that he is going to appear, but as time goes on, you believe it less.

By Thursday at three, there is still no sign of Kevin. "What a rat," says Cathy. "Well, I'm not going to let him ruin your night. I'll be back in a minute."

Cathy comes back jumping up and down. "We have a double date tonight with Mark and his friend Cary, two of the most gorgeous guys in the world. I have to let them know in the next fifteen minutes. What do you say?"

"But suppose Kevin shows up?" you ask.

"Oh, come on," says Cathy, "face the facts. Besides, if you don't go, that blows my date too."

If you say no to Cathy's offer and wait to see if Kevin shows up, turn to page 57.

If you accept the double date, turn to page 60.

You are relieved to see that there is no one at the food table, and you are delighted to discover that dinner is spaghetti and meatballs. As you pile your paper plate with spaghetti, you are thankful that you can look busy by filling up a plate and eating. You know that the more food you have, the longer you can avoid having to deal with the social scene, so you keep piling on the spaghetti. Then you ladle on tons of tomato sauce. You can smell the garlic and the oregano, and you can tell by the thick red texture of the sauce that it's exactly the kind you love.

As you walk slowly back into the living room supporting the bottom of the plate with both hands, you can feel the heat of the spaghetti through the thin cardboard. As you pass a group of people on your way to the couch, the bottom of the plate feels slightly damp. By the time you reach the white velvet couch, you realize what is about to happen; but it is too late. Your scream does nothing more than alert everyone to look in your direction.

Just as you sit down, the plate splits, and enough spaghetti to feed the entire room slithers onto your lap. Thick red sauce oozes onto the pristine white couch and three meatballs bounce across the coffee table.

You have struck out without even going to the ball game.

The End

What could he want? you wonder, hoping that he is about to ask you out.

You step out the door and Jeff puts his hand on your shoulder and looks into your eyes. You were right about his eyes; they *are* blue. You wonder if he can hear your heart pounding.

"The hamburger was perfectly done," he begins. "And the toasted roll was great. It's the new recipe that's the problem."

You look at him in confusion as he takes the uneaten portion of his hamburger from behind his back. "Have a bite," he suggests.

You take a bite and feel the crunch of sand in your teeth.

"Uh-oh," you say, wishing that you would be swallowed up by the earth. Then you explain about the volleyball and your decision to save some of the top burgers. "I'll make you another," you say as you rush inside to warn Cathy to throw away the sandy meat.

"Thanks," he calls after you. "But I think I'll have some popcorn instead."

You fill up a bag to overflowing and pour on extra butter. "I'm really sorry," you say. "The next hamburger's on me."

"Don't worry about it," he says, smiling. *What great dimples,* you think. "Thanks for the popcorn." As he is putting a handful of popcorn into his mouth, you catch sight of B.F. flying straight for Jeff's hand.

(continued on page 55)

"Stop," you scream, not sure if you are talking to the bird or to Jeff. But you are too late. The bird grabs the popcorn from between Jeff's fingers and flies off.

"Ouch," says Jeff when he feels the peck of her beak. Two seconds later you look up and see B.F. about to dive again.

"Drop it," you call, and Jeff tosses the bag into the air. Immediately the sand is filled with birds eating Jeff's popcorn.

"Oh, no," you groan. "I can't believe this is happening."

You quickly pop a hot dog into a bun and rush outside to hand it to Jeff.

"Hey, come on, kid," yells an angry man from line. "I've been waiting for fifteen minutes to get a Coke."

"You working this stand or you working the lifeguard?" yells another.

When Jeff sees you coming, he holds out both hands as if he is holding off the enemy. "Stop where you are," he says. "Please don't come any closer. And whatever you do, don't give me any more food."

Part of you wants to cry, but instead you burst out laughing. You feel as though you are part of an old *I Love Lucy* show—and you are playing the starring role.

"Okay," you say to Jeff. "I'll leave you alone. But you have to promise to give me another chance. I'm not always such a disaster."

(continued on page 56)

"Some other day," says Jeff. And he jogs back to his station, shaking his head.

The rest of the afternoon is hectic, but at least there are no more disasters. At five o'clock you and Cathy close up. The beach is still packed and you are relieved to climb into your car and turn the key. You shift into reverse and step on the accelerator. *Thank heavens this day is over,* you are thinking, when suddenly you crash into a car that is parked across from you. Your eyes fill with tears. *Why can't I do anything right?* you wonder, feeling as though there must be a black cloud following you around.

You get out of the car. Luckily the only damage is a broken right rear taillight on the other car. Bits of red plastic are scattered on the ground. You glance around the parking lot and realize that no one saw you hit the other car.

If you decide that the damage is minimal and you do not have to leave a note, turn to page 59.

If you leave a note on the windshield of the other car, turn to page 62.

"I can't go," you say to Cathy. "I have to give Kevin until the end of the day. Besides, I'd be lousy company."

"Hey, look, I can't tell you what to do, but I really don't understand you," Cathy says. "You've already ruined your night; now you're going to ruin mine as well."

Cathy is furious. For the next hour and a half, she barely says a word. At four-thirty, you can't stand the tension anymore and you tell her if she wants, she can go home. You'll close up.

You are relieved when she goes because you really want to be alone. You keep hoping Kevin will show, even though you have just about given up. Slowly you store the food away, sweep up and finally put the money in the safe.

By five o'clock, you have finished everything, and you can feel your eyes filling with tears. You close up the awning, slam the door and lock up. You wipe the tears from your cheek and walk slowly toward your car. *Well*, you think, *I was all wrong about Kevin and now Cathy is mad at me, too. I've blown everything*.

Just as you are unlocking your door, a blue car screeches to a stop in front of you. Before you have time to think, Kevin jumps out, takes your hands, and twirls you around. He is bursting with excitement.

"I just spent the last two days standing in line," he says. "I almost missed you, I'm flat broke, and I got a speeding ticket on my way here, but *guess*

(continued on page 58)

what? You are about to have the experience of a lifetime! We have front-row seats for the Rolling Stones' concert at the Forum and a special invitation to an after-concert party at a fabulous Beverly Hills mansion. Wear something wonderful. I'll pick you up in an hour."

The End

You look at the broken taillight and decide that the damage couldn't be more than five dollars. You are exhausted and angry and you don't even have a piece of paper in your purse. You drive home.

You fall into bed at nine o'clock, exhausted. At three, you awaken with nightmares and can't get back to sleep. The broken taillight keeps flashing through your mind. At five, you give up trying to sleep and take out an Agatha Christie mystery; but you can't concentrate.

Maybe the people who own the car will come to the beach again tomorrow, you think, and you vow to offer to pay for a new light. Finally you fall asleep.

The next morning there is a note taped to the back door of the hot dog stand. "Please come by my station before work. Jeff."

Whoopee, you think. *I'm about to get my second chance.*

You run across the sand to the lifeguard station, feeling full of energy in spite of your poor night's sleep.

"Hi," you say when Jeff walks toward you. "You're not afraid of me anymore?"

"No," he says. "Not afraid, just disappointed. I was watching you when you left work last night thinking, well, she may be a little dizzy, but she's probably a lot of fun. I've changed my mind. That was my car you rammed."

The End

You stall Cathy for another fifteen minutes, hoping Kevin will appear. While your hands plop hot dogs into buns and popcorn into cups, your eyes dart back and forth from the beach to the parking lot in search of Kevin's curly head and his carefree stroll.

"Time's up," says Cathy. "I've got to call them back. Come on. If you say no we're both going to spend the night alone. Kevin's had his chance. He's not going to show up now."

You realize that you can't stall any longer. "Okay. I'll go," you say, and Cathy rushes off to call the boys.

You and Cathy spend the remaining hour and a half planning what you are going to wear. You decide on your soft blue jumpsuit and your white canvas pumps. Cathy is going to come home with you and try on your ruffly white blouse to wear with her striped peddle pushers. You try to work up some enthusiasm for your double date, but you keep wondering what happened to Kevin.

While you clean the grill, Cathy sweeps the floor. You lock up at five on the dot. Just as you enter the parking lot, a blue car screeches to a halt next to you.

"I got them, I got them," screams Kevin. "I've been standing in line for two days to get us tickets for the Stones' concert tonight. I got the last two." He jumps out of his car and throws his arms around you in a spontaneous hug. You wish you had never been born.

(continued on page 61)

The glow in Kevin's eyes turns to astonishment when you tell him that you can't go. His mouth drops open, and for a minute he can barely talk. Finally he looks at you and shakes his head. "I'm sorry," he says. Then he walks toward the volleyball court.

The last thing you see before you drive away is Kevin talking to one of the girls. She leaps into the air as though she is spiking a ball over the net, but you know she is not practicing her shot.

The End

You decide that you had better leave a note. No matter what the damage is, it's your responsibility to pay for it.

You find a napkin in your purse and write: "To Whom It May Concern: I hit your car and damaged your taillight. Please call 454-0233. Sorry."

You stick the note under the windshield and get back into your car. All you want to do is go home. The whole day has been horrible and you feel like crying.

When you arrive home, you grab a giant bag of corn chips from the cabinet and plop down in front of the television. You have fallen asleep when the phone rings.

"Hi," a male voice says. "I got a note on my car with this number."

"Oh," you say, "you're speaking to the right person. I am really sorry about that."

You arrange to meet in the parking lot at quarter to nine the next morning.

The next day you pull in and see the victimized car. You park and walk toward it. Just then the door opens and Jeff steps out. He looks at you in astonishment. _No way,_ you think. _This is not happening._

"I don't believe it," he says, walking toward you. Then he starts to laugh. "Someone really wants us to get together. It's bigger than both of us," he says. "How about dinner tonight?"

The End

You decide that it would be dishonest to lose intentionally. *Besides,* you think, *it might be kind of fun to beat the hot shot.* The game continues and sure enough, you win. You detect both surprise and admiration in Kevin's green eyes. The two guys look at you in amazement.

"Come on, Kevin, we're in doubles," calls a male voice from the court.

"No way," Kevin shouts back, "I have a rematch to play." He turns to you and says, "I think I'm the one who's been hustled."

"Sorry, Kevin," says the short guy who was watching the game. "I have winners, remember?"

"Oh, yeah. Well, then, can I have a rematch tomorrow? I can't let you off that easily."

"Anytime," you say, enjoying the attention. Your next game ends quickly. You win again. As you are walking back to work, the football type yells to you, "Hey, we're all going for pizza at six. Why don't you join us?"

"Okay. I'll try to make it," you say.

You jog back to the stand and tell Cathy about your new friends and their invitation. You both decide to have pizza with them. You are excited that you have met new people and are already being invited places. The volleyball group seems like fun and the summer is getting better by the hour.

The End

You decide that winning is probably more important to Kevin than it is to you. You know that just a few dumb moves will turn the game around. After intentionally leaving a man open, you are suddenly sorry you did it. You hate losing on purpose. *Cheating to lose is just as bad as cheating to win,* you think. *Any guy that would get really mad about a girl winning isn't worth having anyway.*

Just then a volleyball flies in your direction. Kevin pushes you out of the way and the ball lands on the backgammon board, ruining the game.

What a break, you say to yourself, happy that you are not going to lose dishonestly.

"Too bad," you say. "I really have to be getting back to work anyway. I've been gone a long time."

"If you promise me a rematch, we'll call this one a draw," says Kevin.

"Sure," you say. "How about tomorrow?"

"Hey, Kevin," a girl calls from the court. "Did you figure out anything for all of us to do tonight?"

"Not yet. I'm still working on it," he answers. Then he turns to you as you start walking back. "Listen, why don't you stop by later? We're trying to plan something to do tonight."

"Okay," you say. "I'd be glad to." You can't stop staring at his fantastic green eyes.

When you get back to the stand, you tell Cathy about the invitation.

"Those guys are fun," she says. "I'm definitely up for doing something with them. Hey," she con-

(continued on page 65)

tinues, "didn't you say that your parents were away?"

Hesitantly you answer yes. Cathy suggests that you have a barbecue at your house and invite everyone. The idea sounds exciting, but your parents have made you promise not to have people over; you know that they would kill you if they found out. *How would they find out?* you think. *We don't even know our neighbors.*

If you decide that your parents won't find out and that this would be a great way to meet people, turn to page 66.

If you decide that you cannot break your promise, turn to page 71.

They'll never find out, you decide. "Okay," you say to Cathy. "As long as there aren't too many people."

"Great," Cathy says. "I'll run down and tell them. Be right back."

You are not sure that you are doing the right thing; in fact you know that you are not. But what could happen?

Ten minutes later Cathy returns. "They said that they'll bring the food. Kevin looked pretty happy when I said we were going to your house. I think he's got a crush on you."

You and Cathy decide to close a little bit early and you both drive over to your house. Cathy helps you get the barbecue ready. Then you spend two hours trying to figure out what to wear. You decide on bermuda shorts and a white ruffled blouse. Cathy says that you look great without looking as if you tried to dress up. She borrows a pair of jeans and a purple sweater, trying for the same look.

By eight you are getting very antsy. You are excited, but nervous; if your parents ever found out, you would be grounded forever.

You hear several cars drive up at the same time.

"So, you carry one, you bum!" says a voice. There is laughter, and then a knock.

You rush to answer it. Cathy grabs you.

"Let them wait a minute," she says. "That way they won't think that we're anxiously awaiting their arrival."

(continued on page 67)

You look at Cathy and laugh, thinking about the last two and a half hours during which you have been preparing for and anxiously awaiting their arrival. Cathy slowly walks to the door and opens it. Three guys file in; they are each carrying a case of beer. Your eyes pop. You didn't expect any alcohol. That wasn't part of the bargain.

"Hi! How are you girls tonight!" asks one of the guys.

"Great," Cathy answers.

"You know it's still so hot out it's unbelievable," says another.

The doorbell rings and ten more people walk in, including Kevin. You are suddenly frightened. If your parents knew that you and your friends had brought alcohol into your house, you would be grounded for longer than forever. But you *did* invite them over; how can you tell them to leave? No one would ever talk to you again.

You sit away from the crowd until you finally come up with a brilliant idea. You run into your parents' bedroom and call the operator.

"Can you please call me back? There's something wrong with my phone and I want to check it. Thank you."

You then run back into the kitchen where everyone is standing. The phone rings.

"Hello," you say, picking it up. "Yes. Oh, hi, Mom. Where are you? You're where?" you say, acting surprised. "Oh, nothing's wrong. I'll see you

(continued on page 68)

later." You hang up the phone and look around the room. Everyone has stopped talking and is looking at you.

"Your parents?" Cathy asks.

"They just called from the airport. They're grabbing a cab. They'll be home in an hour. I can't believe it," you say. "They weren't supposed to be back for two days."

"We better clear out," says one of the guys, grabbing the beer.

"I'm really sorry," you say. "I had no idea."

"Don't worry about it," Kevin says. "I have a hibachi at my house. We can stop off and get it and go down to the beach. You can come in my car."

"No," you say. "My parents are expecting me to be here when they arrive."

"You sure?" he says.

"Yeah, thanks anyway."

"Well, thanks for trying," he says. "I'll see you tomorrow for our backgammon game."

As you shut the door, you commend yourself on your performance. No one guessed that you were talking to yourself.

So if everything is so perfect, you think, *why am I standing here alone?*

The End

"Sorry, Tony, but I already have an escort back. I'd beat you anyway," you say.

"Ha!" he says and jogs off.

You climb into the caged cart that Bobby drives. There is only one seat and it's for the driver. You sit cross-legged on the floor. Bobby doesn't say much as he drives. He just stares and smiles at you and eats his ice cream. He never even notices the bush.

"Watch out!" you scream too late. The cart crashes into the bush and Bobby's ice cream ends up all over you.

"I'll have this thing ready to go in a minute," says Bobby, pulling the cart out of the bush.

"Thanks," you say. "But I think I'll walk."

Bobby just sits there looking forlorn and lovesick as he watches you walk back to the cabin, 7-Up squishing in your sneakers, ice cream dripping down your arm.

Tough luck.

The End

You, Tim and Stephen enter the dining room, with Stephen holding your hand. *Maybe California won't be so bad after all,* you think. *Carlos was right about having a good summer.*

"Would you come with me a moment?" a voice says. When you turn around, you get a sick feeling in your stomach. It's Mr. Taylor. And he is talking to you.

You excuse yourself from the table and walk outside with him.

"I can't believe it," he says. "You have not even been here a day and already you've broken two rules. You are the *help.* You do not fraternize with the guests. And you do not eat in their dining room."

And then he says, "I'm sorry, young lady, I thought that you were going to work out. Obviously, I was wrong. I don't think Silverwood is the right place for you. When you turn in your shirts, I will pay you for the morning."

You have been fired after only four hours on the job. Better luck next time.

The End

After thinking about the pros and cons, you decide that you really don't want to take the risk. You made a promise and you have to keep it. You'll have a party some night when your parents are home.

After you close up, you and Cathy walk over to the volleyball court. Soon Kevin comes over to you.

"It's about time you guys closed up. We've been waiting for you. Mark's dad just gave him fifteen free tickets to Disneyland. Okay, everybody, they're here. Let's get going."

He takes your hand and you run together to the parking lot. As you sit in the middle of a carful of people, Kevin leans over and whispers in your ear, "That was the luckiest shot in my life."

The End

"That's a real tempting offer," you say. "But I can't."

Before you have time to explain why, Stephen pulls his brother toward the door. "Come on. Me and Tim Two are hungry."

"See you around," says Tim. You notice how the sun brings out the red streaks in his hair as he walks toward the clubhouse.

I blew it, you think. *I just blew my big chance. Stupid rules.*

For the afternoon activity, you organize a big game of dodge ball. You look for Stephen, hoping Tim will be in tow, but neither one shows up. You divide the ten kids into two groups.

"Form a circle," you tell one group. "Now the rest of you get in the middle." You hand Candy a big rubber ball. She picks it up over her head and throws it into the middle, scattering her opponents.

The kids are screeching and yelling and having a good time when two of the older boys start to play rough. One of them smashes the ball at Candy and she starts to cry. "Both of you leave!" you say to the older boys. You walk over and pick up Candy.

"They giving you trouble?" a male voice says behind you. You turn around. A handsome guy wearing blue jeans and a cowboy hat chases the two boys. They run away laughing.

"Hi," he says. "I'm Peter. I work with the horses. If those kids give you any more trouble, give a yell," he says and walks off.

You put Candy on your shoulders and watch

(continued on page 73)

Peter walk away. *This summer gets better by the minute,* you think.

When the game is over, you walk back toward the crafts cabin, bouncing Candy on your shoulders.

"Yippee!" she yells.

"There you are," says a tall man with a dark beard.

"I was playing games and riding my horse here," Candy says, laughing.

"Well, let's go. Your mother is waiting for you. I'm Mr. Powell," he says, holding out his hand. "I hope I'll see you at Candy's party next Monday."

"Hi," you say, bending down to let Candy off. "I'll let you know tomorrow."

Before going into the cabin, you take one last look for Tim. No luck!

A half hour later, as you are walking to your car to go home, someone taps you on the shoulder. You turn around and practically bump noses with Tim.

"Hi," he says. "I came to thank you for taking such an interest in Stephen. He's been walking around all day with Tim Two on his hand. I haven't seen him so cheerful in a long time. He's in love with you, you know. And he's really proud that he made the puppet himself. Come over here for a minute. My dad would like to meet you."

As you walk toward the tennis court on the far side of the parking lot, you feel as though you are walking on a cloud. You didn't even have to find Tim. He found you.

"I guess I ought to warn you . . ." Tim says.

(continued on page 74)

Oh no, what now? you think. *He's probably going to introduce me to his girlfriend too.*

"It's about my dad."

You are confused. What is he so nervous about? And why should anything about his dad be of any concern to you?

"Well," Tim says, "do you go to the movies a lot?"

Now what? you think. *Is he going to ask me to a movie?*

"Did you see *The Last Moment*?" he says.

"Sure, I loved it," you answer. *What is he talking about?*

"My dad, well . . . my dad played the lead," Tim says. "I just don't want you to be surprised when you meet him."

His dad is . . . Robert Redburn? You can't believe it. You are about to meet a famous movie star. You have seen every movie that he has ever made. He won an Oscar for best actor in *The Last Moment*.

You suddenly get goose bumps. *What do I say to a movie star?*

"Dad, come meet Stephen's friend," Tim calls as you stand by the fence of the tennis court. Then he turns to you. "He asked me who was responsible for Tim Two. I told him I'd bring you over."

Tim's father is even more handsome in tennis shorts than he is in the movies. As he walks over, the lump in your throat grows.

"Nice to meet you," you say.

(continued on page 75)

"The pleasure is mine," he says. "Stephen thinks you are the most wonderful person who ever lived."

"Don't forget, Dad," Stephen yells from the court.

"Oh yes. Stephen has asked me to invite you to our party next Monday. If you give Tim your address, I'll have someone pick you up at home."

The lump in your throat turns into a volleyball. The club is closed on Mondays and you are free. Then you remember: next Monday is Candy's birthday party. She really wants you, and fifty dollars is a lot of money.

If you go to the Redburn party, turn to page 80.

If you take the job, turn to page 87.

You are not really all that concerned about Mr. Redburn. In fact, he has not even greeted you. *He probably doesn't even remember who I am,* you think. But you cannot bring yourself to walk away from the glitter of a Hollywood party.

For the next hour you wander around, listening to conversations, watching flirtations, and eating non-stop. The food is fabulous; the people are a floor show; the musical entertainment is like something out of a TV variety program. But no one talks to you.

As the evening wears on, the guests become noisier. There is hysterical laughter coming from everywhere, and you cannot figure out what anyone is laughing at. Several guests, in their silk dresses and luau shirts, either are pushed or jump into the pool. Others, laughing, join them, fully clothed.

You try to laugh, but it is hard to laugh when you are standing by yourself. You wish you had brought your car so that you could leave without telling anyone. But you arrived in the chauffeured limousine and have no way to go home until the end of the party. You feel trapped. You walk back to the corner of the yard and lean against the eucalyptus tree where you first saw Tim.

You wish you had gone with him.

The End

You cancel afternoon recreation and spend the next two hours talking to staff members. You discover that Carlos has worked at Silverwood for three years and everybody loves him; he is always helping people out.

The tennis coach tells you about the time Carlos fixed her car when the carburetor was stuck. The cook remembers when Carlos brought him a bag of home-grown tomatoes and zucchini. One of the men who parks cars tells you about how Carlos helped him clean up a gallon of oil that spilled all over the lot. You think about the support he gave you on your first day of work and the pile of wood scraps that turned into boats for the kids.

Every single person you talk to is furious at Taylor. By three o'clock, you have gotten the support of the whole staff. They all agree to quit if Taylor won't rehire Carlos.

At three-thirty, you all meet outside Taylor's office. You have agreed to be the spokesperson. You walk into his office alone and tell him that his entire staff is going to quit unless he puts Carlos back on the payroll. He laughs.

"Who do you think you are, Wonder Woman?" he says.

"I think I am a human being, the same as Carlos," you say.

"I cannot hire him back. He broke the rules."

You are ready to explode. But instead, you speak calmly. "We realize that he broke the rules, and that

(continued on page 78)

you were only doing your job. But we're hoping that you'll reconsider.''

"It's my job," says Taylor, "to see that the staff respects the rules. If I let Carlos get away with it, I'll be setting a precedent. I'm sorry, but I can't change my mind."

You can tell that Taylor doesn't believe that the whole staff is willing to walk out over this issue.

"Mr. Taylor," you say, "I would like to show you something." You open the door. Seventeen staff members are standing there. Taylor turns pale. He knows that the club cannot function without a staff.

"Well," he says, "maybe if I can get a promise from all of you that you will not consider it a precedent."

Everyone agrees quickly.

"All right," he says. "I'll rehire Carlos. Now get back to work."

"Not until you call Carlos," you say. You go back into the office and listen while Taylor tells Carlos the good news. You try to control yourself, but your smile explodes. You gallop out of the office and down to the parking lot, followed by seventeen friends, all cheering and congratulating each other.

After a few minutes, Peter tosses his cowboy hat in the air and says, "Hey, we'd better get back to work. We might get fired." Everyone laughs.

The End

Tony parks his beat-up old Mustang in back of the theater. As you are walking toward the front door, Tony has a brainstorm.

"Look," he says, "everyone is coming out from the last show. I bet we could get in the back door without anyone noticing."

You've never snuck in anywhere before, and you don't like the idea. Tony, however, has made up his mind. He grabs your hand and heads toward the back door where everyone is exiting. *What a romantic date*, you think. But then, you knew better than to expect anything normal with Tony.

He pulls you through the crowd and you sit down quickly.

"We made it," he says. "I knew it would work."

Your heart is pounding and your hands are sweaty. A man walks toward you.

"Excuse me, kids. We have a front door for a reason. I would advise you to leave immediately before I call the police." Everyone is staring at you. When Tony takes your hand to lead you out, you pull your hand away.

"Let's go to another movie," he says.

"Thanks, but I'd like to go home," you say.

On the drive home, you don't say a word. All you can think about is the fact that you have blown your chances for a date with Peter.

The End

You cannot resist the offer. A party filled with movie stars. You have been in Los Angeles for only two weeks and already you have been invited to the home of a movie star!

You spend two hours Monday morning trying to figure out what to wear to a fabulous Hollywood party. You don't know a soul who has ever been to one. Do you wear shorts? It *is* the middle of the afternoon. No, you decide; something with a skirt. Or maybe a silk jumpsuit or sequined or satin pants. You don't own any. The only place you've ever seen things like that is in magazines or on television.

You spread everything you own onto your bed and floor and push aside the awful stuff. You are finally left with three skirts and a pileful of tops, most of them three years old. You decide on a navy cotton skirt with a huge white floral pattern and a white blouse with a high ruffled neck. *Not bad,* you think when you try it on. *Not Hollywood, but not bad.*

Then you take out some makeup—blue shadow, gold, lavender. First you line your eyes in black; then you take off the black and try dark brown. You wonder if there will be swimming; you are certain that every movie star has a pool in the backyard. If you put on makeup, you won't be able to go swimming; your hair would be a mess when you got it wet.

Finally after hours of agony, you are ready. At three o'clock your doorbell rings and you open it,

(continued on page 81)

expecting to see Tim. Instead, a man in a chauffeur's uniform says, "How do you do, ma'am. I'm Harris." Harris ushers you into the back seat of a monstrous limousine where there is a small tray with cold shrimp, two kinds of cheeses and an iced bottle of Coke.

You have eaten only two shrimp when the car pulls into the circular drive in front of the Redburn house. The driveway is lined with Rolls Royces, sleek sports cars, and one white and silver vehicle that looks like something that has dropped in from outer space. There is not a Datsun or Honda in sight.

Most of the guests are around the swimming pool. You have never seen so many beautiful women or spectacular-looking men in your life. As you are wandering around, gaping at the many familiar faces, someone drops a lei of real orchids around your neck. There are four roving musicians playing ukuleles, and every few yards someone else offers you exotic foods from a tray—pineapples wrapped in bacon and things called rumaki and teriyaki chicken, and beef on a skewer.

You are absolutely overwhelmed by the lavish floral and plant decorations. You feel as though you are in a tropical forest. As you are walking toward the buffet table, you catch sight of Tim in the corner of the yard. He is leaning against a eucalyptus trunk, sketching. You notice that Mr. Redburn is walking toward him from the other direction.

You and Mr. Redburn reach Tim almost simulta-

(continued on page 82)

neously. Before you have a chance to greet them, Mr. Redburn says to his son, "Put that danged sketchbook away. I told you not to take it out at parties. I'm sick and tired of being embarrassed by you."

Several nearby heads turn to look. "Oh," says one star whose face you know but whose name you can't remember, "it's just Bob and that arty kid of his at it again. The kid likes to stand around at parties and draw pictures and it drives Bob crazy."

You look at Tim. There are tears in his eyes and his lips are curled in anger and hurt. "Excuse me," he says to you, refusing to look at his father. "I have to leave."

If you tell Tim you'd like to leave with him, turn to page 93.

If you are concerned about insulting Mr. Redburn, turn to page 76.

"I can't," you tell Tony. "I have to babysit for my brother tonight."

"Too bad," says Tony. "You don't know what you're missing."

You smile. He is nice, but you are hoping that one of these days Peter notices that you are a girl as well as a children's counselor. Meanwhile you intend to keep Tony as a friend—nothing more.

The next two weeks fly by. You and Tony and Bobby become fast friends. They both keep asking you out, but you manage to joke your way out of a straight answer. Peter, meanwhile, shows up for planning sessions and is hardly ever around after work when you, Tony and Bobby go out for ice cream sundaes or pizza or an occasional movie. Peter spends most of his time with the horses, even after hours.

The night before All Kids' Day you cannot sleep. At first you think it is because you are so excited; you have, after all, spent most of the summer planning this day. But then you realize that there is something eerie about the night. Winds are howling through the trees, rattling the panes in your windows, tearing off branches and dropping them on your roof. *The famous Santa Ana Winds,* you think. *Warm and powerful.* You have read about them, but this is the first time you have heard them.

The winds are still blowing when you leave in the morning, and the road into the canyon where the

(continued on page 84)

Silverwood Club is located is littered with palm leaves. As you drive into the parking lot, trying to think of some crafts project that will utilize all those leaves, something drops onto your car roof from the shade tree near where you park.

You jump out to see if there is any damage and Tony is standing on your car with a megaphone.

"Welcome to the first annual Creepy Kids' Day, a program of outstanding events for rotten kids. The first order of the day is a one-legged race. All contestants report to me in the infirmary for their amputations. The second event is a Quicksand Contest. First one down wins. And last, the Water Polo Championships at three o'clock. The first team to drown the other wins a trophy."

"Tony," you say, "you're a nut. That's probably why I love you."

"And I love you," says Tony. "So let's live happily ever after."

Peter arrives at that point and wishes you both happiness. "But first," he says. "let's get this show on the road."

There are eight staff members and together you work out who will be overseeing each event. By the time you are finished, the kids have begun to arrive. By ten o'clock, there are 68 kids raring to get started.

The morning is a smash success. Bobby gives rides to the smallest kids in his caged golf cart, and there are tournaments and contests everywhere you

(continued on page 85)

look. For the final session of the morning, you take the middle group up a grassy hill in the middle of the golf course, and you all spend the next half hour rolling down, climbing up and rolling down again.

"Last roll before lunch," you call from the top of the hill. You are enjoying yourself as much as the kids when you look out across the canyon from your hilltop and discover that there are billows of black smoke in the distance.

Oh no, you think. *The canyon is burning.* You estimate that the fire is about ten miles away and you wonder if the club is in danger.

"Last one to the pool has to clean up after lunch," you shout, and you run as fast as you can to tell Tony and Bobby, who are in charge of pool games.

The guys take off in Bobby's cart to see the smoke for themselves, while you sing with the kids at the side of the pool. Two minutes later they return.

"No problem," says Tony. "It's just a brush fire. They'll have that thing under control long before it gets here."

"Not with these winds," says Bobby. "We've got to get everybody out before it gets dangerous."

"Hey, don't panic," Tony says. "Just calm down. If we're really in trouble, the firemen will come and tell us to evacuate. Meanwhile, let's get on with the program."

(continued on page 86)

"Yeah," calls one of the kids. "We're hungry. Let's eat lunch."

Bobby turns to you. "I've seen these fires before. They move fast. We've got to get everyone out of here now."

"Boo," scream the kids.

If you think Bobby has panicked and you would rather go with Tony's more reasonable proposal, turn to page 91.

If you agree with Bobby, turn to page 100.

You have been having car problems, so at three o'clock Monday afternoon, you are waiting for Mrs. Powell to pick you up. Mr. Powell is at the door when you answer the bell. You follow him to a shining black and tan Rolls Royce. Mrs. Powell is sitting in the passenger seat. You put your large paper bag in the trunk and climb into the back seat.

"Robert has a meeting to go to and I have things to do," Mrs. Powell says. "Our cook will take care of dinner. The rest is up to you and the musician, Tom."

"That's fine," you say. You have thought up enough activities to last at least ten hours, even though the party is only for three.

After riding for ten minutes, you pull into a road marked with a large sign that reads, Powell Grove. You are overwhelmed by the lavish avocado grove that surrounds you. The branches are weighted with deep dark avocados, hidden among the lush green leaves.

When you walk up the stone path toward the house, Candy comes bounding out the door.

"Why don't you help me empty out my bag before all your friends get here?" you say to Candy. "We're going to have to set up some pots outside for tie dyeing."

You are yanked through the house to the patio. You and Candy take all of the old white T-shirts out of your bag and put them on the ground.

"Hi!" a deep voice bellows from directly behind you. You turn around to face a blue shirt on a very

(continued on page 88)

tall person. Your eyes move up to a dark-com-
plected face and deep brown eyes. He is carrying a
guitar. "I'm Tom," he says. "Can I give you a
hand?"

You feel like a Munchkin from *The Wizard of Oz*
standing next to him. "You sure can," you say, as
you introduce yourself.

Then the two of you, trailed by a bouncing
Candy, set up three large pots of water and fill them
with different-colored dyes. The kids have started
to arrive, and soon you are surrounded by fifteen
bright-eyed faces.

"What are we doing?" one little girl asks.

"Can I make myself blue?" a red-haired boy
shouts.

You hand each kid a T-shirt and take out a box of
rubber bands. You then demonstrate how to tie
the rubber bands on the T-shirts to get different
designs.

"Do I get to make one?" Tom asks.

"I don't think they make shirts big enough for
you. But be my guest," you say, handing him a
shirt.

"I can't do it!" one dark-haired girl with a pony-
tail exclaims. You patiently show her how to use the
rubber bands.

"Don't dip your whole arm in!" you say to the
boy who wanted to turn himself blue. Everyone
laughs.

As each shirt is finished, you and Tom hang it on
a line that Mrs. Powell has put up. Next, you gather

(continued on page 89)

everyone for a scavenger hunt. You split the party into three groups and hand each group a list.

"The group with the most items wins. Be back in one hour and don't leave the block." Fifteen screaming and giggling kids charge out the door.

"That's great," Tom says. "You really came up with some fantastic ideas."

"You're on stage next," you say to Tom. "I'm pooped already. "Eight-year-olds are definitely full of energy."

"I'll play a little before dinner," Tom says.

"Sounds great!" you say. "Where are you from?" you ask Tom, noticing the slight slant of his brown eyes and a faint accent in his deep voice.

"The Philippines. Do you like to sing?" he asks.

"I love to, especially when I'm playing the piano," you answer.

"You play? That's great," he says. "We'll move the group into the piano room and do some duets. How 'bout it?"

"Okay," you agree.

For the next half hour you and Tom sit and chat about school and summer. You are fascinated by the deep resonant tone of his voice. You cannot believe it when you discover that he goes to your high school.

Your peace is shattered when the troops return.

"We have the most!" a boy yells, running into the house. He is soon followed by the others.

After tallying up the points and deciding the winners, you direct the kids into the other room.

(continued on page 90)

"Old MacDonald" is the first song that Tom plays. The kids sing and laugh loudly.

"For the next song," Tom announces, "we will have a piano player too," he says, smiling at you.

You and Tom are a terrific duo. Your instruments blend, and so do your voices.

After an hour of singing, the kids are marched into the dining area to eat and open presents. By seven o'clock, the parents start to arrive, and by seven-thirty, all of the kids have gone.

"I'll drive you home now," Mrs. Powell says. "Thanks, you were terrific." She puts her arm around your shoulder. You smell alcohol on her breath. When she moves to the table to pick up her purse, you notice a slight sway in her walk.

If you ask Tom for a ride home, even though you know he lives in the opposite direction, turn to page 16.

If you let Mrs. Powell drive you home, turn to page 97.

Tony's reasoning makes sense, and you don't want to panic the kids unnecessarily. Besides, the Los Angeles fire department can handle brush fires; they've had a lot of experience.

"Okay, you guys," you say to the kids. "Let's spread the blankets and have some lunch."

"You're making the wrong decision," says Bobby. "But at least if we're eating lunch together, we'll all be in the same spot when it comes time to evacuate."

"*If* it comes time to evacuate, Bobby. You're such a worrier," says Tony.

"I'm going to go over to the barn and get Peter to join us," says Bobby, and he takes off in his cage.

You are passing out the fruit and brownies for dessert about an hour later when you notice that the smell of fire in the air has intensified. Then, before you know it, the sky turns dark and sparks and ashes are flying all over. It all seems to have happened in about five minutes. You have no time to calmly load up the cars. Although you cannot see it, you know that the fire is close and everyone has got to be out as quickly as possible.

You pack each car with frightened kids and try not to show how terrified you are. You realize that your terror is not for yourself but for the young lives you are responsible for. Luckily, Tony and Bobby are driving station wagons. They each drive off with fifteen kids.

The remaining 38 kids are squashed into the other four cars. As you caravan through the canyon,

(continued on page 92)

sparks and billows of smoke make the driving treacherous. There is still no sign of the fire, but you are certain that it must be close. You have decided that you will meet at a schoolyard that is far from the canyon and out of the fire area.

By the time your car arrives at the schoolyard, Tony has organized a huge game of dodge ball, and Bobby is calling the parents to come pick up their children. You are standing alone, exhausted and frightened from the experience, when Peter comes over to you. He has just emptied his car of the last load of kids.

"If anyone asks for me, tell them I've gone back for the horses," he tells you.

"You can't go back in there," you say. "The fire is too close."

"I can't *not* go back," he says. "Those four horses have to be led out by hand. I'll try to walk them out two at a time. It's only a mile, and I can drive one way. It shouldn't take long. I think there's still time."

_____

If you tell Peter you will go with him, turn to page 102.

If you try to talk him out of it, turn to page 108.

"Wait a minute, Tim," you call. "Can you drive me home?"

"Don't you want to stay and meet the stars?"

"No," you answer. "Not after what I heard."

"Come on then," he says. He smiles shyly. "I'm sorry I was so rude, but my father does this to me every time."

"You shouldn't let him get to you like that."

"I can't help it. I can never please him. I'm just not like him, and he doesn't understand that."

"But you shouldn't have to be. You are your own person—and not only that," you add after you have been driving for a while and leafing through his sketch pad, "you are a fabulous artist. Have you ever thought of getting a job doing animation? Your characters are great."

"You really think I'm good?" he asks, looking at you with his deep brown eyes.

"Of course you are," you say, as he pulls into your driveway.

He walks you to your door. You stand for a moment, hoping he will ask you out. He only smiles. *Maybe he's too shy,* you think.

If you ask him to a barbecue that you've been invited to, turn to page 104.

If you simply say goodnight, turn to page 107.

"Okay, kids," you say after introductions. "I'm going to need your help."

You ask them to follow you to your car. There you open the trunk and pull out three bags filled with old socks. They carry the bags back to the arts-and-crafts cabin, asking you what the socks are for.

"We're going to make puppets," you say. You put your hand into one of the socks and make a mouth with your fingers. Then, talking in a squeaky voice, you say, "Good idea. I'm tired of being bunched up in that bag. Give me some eyes and some hair." You make the puppet bite the little blond girl's nose and the kids laugh.

They are delighted with your idea and together you begin to create puppets out of socks. Before long, there are fifteen kids, yanking on your arms, legs and hair.

One little girl named Candy puts long yellow braids and bangs on her puppet, to match her own blond braids and bangs. Then she runs off to show her mother the "Candy puppet."

Candy comes back with her mother just before noon.

"I'm Mrs. Powell," the woman says. There is a faint smell of alcohol on her breath. "Candy's puppet is wonderful. You are obviously a very talented young lady. Next Monday is Candy's birthday and I would love it if you would organize and run activities during the party. I will pay you fifty dollars for three hours of activities. I hope you'll say yes."

(continued on page 95)

"Please, please, please," begs Candy, pulling on your arm.

"I'd like to do it," you say. "And Monday the club is closed. But I have to check with my mom first. I'll let you know."

As Mrs. Powell and Candy leave, you notice that everyone is gone except for one boy named Stephen. He is sitting with a sock on his lap. He has done nothing with it.

"I can't do it," Stephen says.

"Sure you can," you say. "First glue on some eyes."

As Stephen tries to put glue onto a circle of white felt, you realize that there is something wrong with his coordination. He drops the glue and it spills all over the floor.

"Oh, no," he says and starts to cry. "I can't do anything right." He runs toward the door; you notice that he has a severe limp.

"Let's use the glue from the floor to put on the eyes," you say.

You and Stephen work slowly. His right hand is disabled and he can work only with his left hand.

You patiently show him how to manage each step, letting him do the work himself.

It is almost one o'clock when you finally finish. Stephen giggles as he puts his left hand into the puppet.

"Hi, my name is Tim," says the puppet.

"Well, hello there," you answer. "You're a fine-looking fellow, Tim."

(continued on page 96)

"Why, thank you," says a male voice. You look up to see a head of curly reddish-brown hair and the smiling brown eyes of a boy about your age.

"She wasn't talking to you," says Stephen, opening and closing his puppet's mouth. "I'm Puppet Tim. My name is Tim Two."

"I'm his brother Tim," says the boy to you.

"I'm sorry. I kept him too long," you say.

"Hey, don't worry about it," says Tim, sitting down next to his brother. "You're late because you were making a puppet for Stephen."

"Oh, no. I did it myself," says Stephen.

"He really did. I just helped out a little," you say.

"Then maybe I can help you out," says Tim. "Let me buy you lunch."

You look at your watch. The recreation session is due to begin in ten minutes. Besides, you remember that you are not allowed in the guest dining room.

But Tim is the first person your own age that you've met since you moved to California. And besides, he has the darkest brown eyes you have ever seen. And on top of all that, you are starving.

If you tell Tim that you will have a quick lunch with them, turn to page 70.

If you explain that you can't go, turn to page 72.

You decide that even though you are nervous, you don't want to insult Mrs. Powell.

"Goodbye, kiddo," you say to Candy. "Nice meeting you, Tom. I hope we see each other again some time." You follow Mrs. Powell to the Rolls, climb in the front seat and put your seat belt on.

Mrs. Powell misses the ignition the first time she tries to put the key in. Your muscles tighten and you take a deep breath.

"So how do you like being mommy to fifteen eight-year-olds?" she asks you.

"It was fun," you say. "But I'm glad that Tom was there also."

"Well, my daughter's friends are always having parties. I'll be sure to recommend you." The car is weaving back and forth.

"That's fantastic," you say. *But get me home first,* you think.

When you reach the main road, Mrs. Powell cuts in front of a car and shoots into the left lane. You hold your breath and clench your fists. She keeps changing lanes unnecessarily and driving much too fast.

I don't care how many recommendations she gives, nothing is worth this, you think. You are holding onto the door. Every time she stops you find your foot pressing against the floor. "There's a stop sign," you yell. It's too late; she goes through it.

"Mrs. Powell," you say, "you must be awfully tired. Why don't you pull over and let me drive?" you say, tears in your eyes.

(continued on page 98)

"Nonsense," she says. "I'm perfectly fine. Besides, no one but Mr. Powell and me drives this car."

There is nothing you can do. You are clenching the seat when you pull in your driveway. You jump out of the car.

"Good night, honey," Mrs. Powell says. "Thanks."

You cannot say a word. You nod and run toward your door. You lie in bed for an hour before you are calm. *I will never get in a car with her again,* you think.

For three days after the party you don't see Candy or her mother. While you are setting up arts and crafts on Friday, a familiar voice calls your name.

"You forgot your party favors when you left," Candy says. She hands you a bag with candy and a noisemaker. "What are we doing today?"

You pick her up and twirl her in the air. "We're making a collage," you say. "And you can be my assistant."

For the next week, Candy is dropped off bright and early every morning by her mother and picked up at four by her mother and father. In the afternoon, Mrs. Powell always has the same look and the same walk as she did the day she drove you home. You check each day to make sure that Mr. Powell is driving.

One day you and your assistant Candy are clean-

(continued on page 99)

ing up spilled paint-water when Mrs. Powell stumbles in.

"Come on, Candy. It's time to leave now. Home time!" she yells. You take Candy's hand. You are at least five feet away from Mrs. Powell and you can smell the alcohol.

"Where's Mr. Powell?" you ask.

"Who knows," she says. "I really don't care!" She reaches for Candy's hand but misses.

You pull Candy close to you, squeezing her hand. "Who's driving?" you ask.

"What do you mean, who's driving? I am. Who do you think?!"

There is no way that you are going to let Candy get in that car with her mother.

"Candy," you say, "we're having spaghetti for dinner tonight. Do you want to come and sleep over?"

"Can I, Mom, can I?" she says, jumping up and down.

"Yes. I guess so. I came all the way and . . . oh, go ahead," she says.

You write down your home phone number and hand it to Mrs. Powell. When she turns to leave, she bumps into the doorway.

If you offer to drive her home, turn to page 106.

If you call a cab for her, turn to page 110.

"Sorry, Tony. I'm with Bobby. I think we've got to get out of here now."

"I'll get everyone to meet in the parking lot," says Bobby as he takes off in his cart. "Load up these kids and get them out."

You ship out the first group in three cars and tell them to resume their activities at a schoolyard that you know is in a safe zone.

When Bobby returns with his cage filled with kids, you and he engineer the evacuation. You watch as he hugs and jokes with the kids who are frightened.

"Okay, pal," he says to one girl who is clearly on the verge of tears. "I am putting you in charge of the Get-Home-Safe Committee." And he hands her a file of members' addresses and phone numbers. It had never occurred to you that these kids would have to be delivered home, or that at the least, their parents would have to be called. The little girl smiles at Bobby and hangs on tightly to the box.

"Line up for your piggyback rides," he calls to the younger kids. They laugh as he dumps them into the car.

You watch Bobby as he sees to it that every kid is loaded into an evacuation vehicle. He is smiling and joking with them, but you can see by his body movements that he is moving fast and efficiently. His voice is strong, reassuring and tender, all at the same time.

As the last carful of kids pulls out and leaves you and Bobby to gather up the remaining equipment,

(continued on page 101)

you hear fire engines racing down the main road. You can smell the fire, and the air has turned gray with soot. An occasional spark flies by you in the wind as you jump into Bobby's cage to have a last look at the fire's progress.

Together you stand in astonishment at the top of the hill. The fire is less than a mile away. "Thank God you were strong," you say to Bobby as he races the cart back to the parking lot. "If we had waited until now, we might not have had time to get everyone out."

Bobby walks you to your car. "I'll follow you out," he says. "Fires are unpredictable. Sometimes a spark can cause a whole new area to burst into flame."

Before you get in, you look into Bobby's eyes. How blue they are. Somehow you never noticed before. You wonder if that floppy piece of hair always sat in the middle of his forehead like that.

Spontaneously, you reach up, pull his face to yours and give him a quick kiss. "I'll see you later," you say, wondering how you missed seeing his inner strength and tenderness. You climb in and drive off. In your rearview mirror you see Bobby galloping toward his car like a horse. *How cute,* you think, knowing that you and Bobby have a lot of catching up to do.

The End

"I'm coming with you," you tell Peter. "Two of us can do it in one trip."

"Are you sure?" he says.

"I'm sure," you answer.

You drive into the canyon road in silence. The smoke is even worse than before. It is one o'clock in the afternoon on a sunny day, and the canyon is shrouded in darkness. Even the headlights on the car do not penetrate the gloom.

Somehow Peter finds the club turnoff and drives to the barn. There you swiftly blindfold the horses and untie them. They are shrieking and twisting and yanking their necks. It is nearly impossible to get them to walk and each of you is trying to lead two of them across the club grounds and out of the canyon.

Even before you get to the road, you see the flames. They are blocking the route out.

"Do you know how to turn on the lawn sprinklers?" you ask Peter. "It may be our only hope."

Peter ties the horses, whinnying and bucking, to some trees; and then, together, you run to turn on the sprinklers. When you return, you walk through the gentle spray, hand in hand, frightened but hopeful. You decide to camp out by the swimming pool, knowing that the buildings could easily catch a spark and burn up. Peter tethers the horses near one of the sprinklers.

As you sit by the pool, you cannot see the fire, but you can hear its roar as it sweeps through the nearby fields. Then you see a burst of flame as the

(continued on page 103)

barn catches fire. Suddenly two other small buildings explode into orange flames.

You can hear the constant noise of sirens, but you realize that the firemen are saving people's houses, not their clubs. You and Peter, tears streaming down your faces, clutch each other's hands as though your lives depended upon your connection. You stare at the burning buildings, barely talking. Words seem so meaningless at a time like this.

The three buildings become smoldering ruins in less than two hours and the Santa Anas carry the fire into the next canyon. The wet grounds are spared.

When you finally realize that you are out of danger, you sit down in one of the pool chairs and close your eyes. The roar of the fire and the crackling of the burning buildings is echoing in your head when you feel Peter's hand on your shoulder. He slips his other hand under your head and presses his lips to yours. Soon, you are locked in an embrace, fused by the passion of a terrifying afternoon together. You have shared an experience that neither of you will ever forget, and you both know that this is only the beginning.

The End

You meet Tim in the beach parking lot and together you walk down to the crowd of people huddled around a barbecue. Tim has brought two steaks and you have brought some soft drinks. The air is cold and you begin to shiver.

"Take my coat," Tim insists. He puts his big warm jacket around your shoulders and you sit down near a dwindling fire.

"I'll go put food on," he says and walks toward the barbecue. As you watch him walk off, he turns and smiles at you. You love his smile, and those brown eyes knock you out.

While Tim is cooking the steaks, you see Peter, one of the guys you work with at the club. You have never really talked to him; he always seems to be surrounded by girls. Now he is walking directly toward you. You can feel your heart speed up.

"Well, hello there," Peter says. "This fire seems to be dying. Let's go find some firewood." He holds out his hand to help you up.

You look at his tan face, his streaked hair, his strong, square jaw. *He looks more gorgeous than ever before,* you think. Then you remember that Tim is over at the barbecue cooking your dinner. You can't just walk off with Peter; Tim is your date. But when you look at Peter, nothing else seems to matter. Besides, it's only to get some firewood.

If you go with Peter, turn to page 112.

If you wait for Tim, turn to page 114.

You've made a promise, and it's your responsibility to get to the boat on time. You call a cab. It's five past eight when you pull up to the boat. The meter reads $22.50. You hand the driver $25 and jump out of the car.

Tom runs over and greets you. He has on black pants, a white shirt and a black bow tie. He takes your hand and brings you inside. You begin by playing "Back in the U.S.S.R." by the Beatles, and you finish three hours later with a medley of Peter, Paul and Mary songs.

The two of you are a smash hit. By the end of the night, you have four offers for other parties. The hostess gives you each a bonus of fifteen dollars, and you are both flying as you walk out the door.

"We were fantastic!" Tom says and he hugs you. "We are some team, and I'd like to make it more than just work. How about dinner tomorrow night?"

"Sure," you say as you look way up into his dark eyes. "I'd love it."

Hmm, you think as you walk hand in hand toward his car. *I wonder how you kiss somebody who's so tall.* You smile in anticipation, knowing you will find out soon.

The End

"Candy," you say, "will you go get us a couple of Cokes?"

"Sure," she says and runs out the door.

"Mrs. Powell," you say, "I can't let you drive home."

"What do you mean, you can't let me drive home? Who says that you have any say in the matter?"

"I do," you say. "You're in no shape to drive that car. Let me drive it."

"You're not driving my car!" she yells.

"If you won't let me drive you home in *your* car, then I'll take you home in *my* car," you say.

"Well," she says, "if it would make you feel better. But I'm really fine."

When Candy returns with the Cokes, you take her hand and walk toward your car. Candy jumps in the back and Mrs. Powell sits in the front.

You drop Mrs. Powell off.

"Are we having meatballs too?" Candy says.

You reach out and grab her hand, squeezing it tightly. "We sure are," you say, tears rolling down your cheeks.

I was there this time, you think. *But what about next time?*

The End

The next two weeks pass very slowly. The weather is lousy and the club is not very crowded. Stephen has come to crafts a few times, but there's been no sign of Tim. You have decided that it was good that you didn't ask him to the barbecue. *He would probably have said no,* you think.

On Sunday night you are walking toward your car, relieved that the next day is Monday, your day off. A car screeches into the lot.

"I did it!" Tim yells, jumping out of his car. "I got a job with Disney." He runs over and hugs you.

"I owe it all to you," he says. "I'm only working as an apprentice right now, but my boss likes my work and says that if I work really hard, I have a good chance of promotion."

"I told you you were great!" you say. "That's fantastic."

"Come on," he says. "Let's go celebrate. Jump in. I'm going to take you for the best dinner you've ever had."

The End

"Peter, please," you say, grabbing his arm. "Don't go back in there."

"I couldn't live with myself if something happened and I didn't even try," he says.

All afternoon, as you wait anxiously for Peter, smoke is billowing into the sky from the direction of Silverwood.

You are sobbing as you drive home, frightened for Peter, terrified by the whole experience. On a hunch, you drive along the boulevard where the canyon road turns in. You are stopped by the police about a half mile from the road and told that cars can go no further. You park and start to walk. Then you run. You can barely breathe when you arrive at the turnoff. Your eyes are clouded with tears. Suddenly you hear someone calling your name. You turn to see Peter sitting at the edge of an empty lot. Two horses are grazing behind him. You rush into his arms.

"They wouldn't let me go back for the other two," he says tearfully. "Maybe they'll make it on their own."

You hug Peter, hoping to give him strength, wanting to help him through his agony. Your cheeks touch and your tears mingle. For a long time neither one of you moves.

"I'm glad you came," he says finally. "I needed someone."

He lifts your face and kisses you gently on the lips.

The End

You decide that if you race out the door as soon as your mother arrives, you'll make it on time.

At a quarter to eight, however, your mother calls to tell you that she won't be home for a couple of hours. You call a cab. By eight o'clock it has still not arrived.

The phone rings at eight-ten.

"Where are you?" Tom yells into the phone. "I can't believe that you're home."

You explain what happened, but Tom does not seem to be listening. "Forget it!" he says. "Don't come at all. It's too late!" He hangs up.

I really messed that one up, you think, tears streaming down your cheeks.

The End

"You want to come make a phone call with me?" you say to Candy.

"Sure," she says.

"I'm calling a cab for you, Mrs. Powell. You are not going to drive." You take Candy's hand and walk out the door.

When you return to the cabin, Mrs. Powell is gone. You run out to the parking lot but her car is nowhere in sight.

"You looking for Candy's mom?" Carlos calls out to you. "She just left."

You look up into the sky, trying to keep the tears from rolling down your cheeks. "Come on, Candy," you say, putting your arm around her shoulder. "We've got a lot of cooking ahead of us."

Your stomach feels weak and the thought of food nauseates you.

"I'm starved!" Candy announces.

After dinner, you and Candy watch *M.A.S.H.* on TV. Candy laughs when Klinger puts on a wedding dress, but you find yourself crying. You give Candy a big kiss when you put her to sleep in your bed.

"Sleep tight," you say and you walk back into the living room. You jump when the phone rings a few minutes later.

"This is St. Thomas' Hospital," says a woman's voice. "We have a woman here and we found this phone number in her pocket."

"What happened? Is she okay?" you ask.

The woman informs you that Mrs. Powell has a broken hip and multiple abrasions. "She is lucky to

(continued on page 111)

be alive," the woman continues. "Fortunately no one was in the car with her. The passenger seat was crushed."

You give the woman Mrs. Powell's name and address.

"When Mr. Powell gets there," you say, "give him this phone number. Their daughter is with me."

When you hang up the phone, you put your head down. It is throbbing. Your whole body is shaking as you walk into your room, pull the covers around Candy and kiss her on the forehead.

The End

I'll only be gone a minute, you think. "Okay," you say, taking his hand and letting him pull you up.

As you are walking down the beach, you glance into Peter's eyes. "Are you cold?" he asks.

"No," you say, feeling Tim's jacket on your shoulders.

You and Peter pick up wood as you walk along the beach. You chat about work. "It's a beautiful night," Peter says.

"It sure is," you say, wishing that this walk would never end. The moon is shining on the ocean and the night is perfect. *It's like a fairy tale,* you think.

"This is probably enough. Here, let me carry it back," Peter says, taking the wood from you. His hand touches your arm and you feel a tingling throughout your body.

When you get back, there are only a few people left on the beach. You have obviously been gone longer than you realized.

"Thanks for helping," Peter says as he walks toward a small group of people.

You look around for Tim. He is nowhere in sight. You are standing alone when you notice a paper plate by the spot where you were first sitting with Tim. You pick up a note that is sitting on top of a cold steak.

> I'm sure you'll have more fun with your friend. Enjoy the steak.
>
> Tim

(continued on page 113)

You look over at Peter. He is standing with his arm around a girl. Holding the note, you walk toward your car. You can feel tears building. By the time you reach your car, they are rolling down your cheeks.

Some fairy tale, you think.

The End

"I can't," you say. "My dinner is being cooked."

"Okay," Peter says. "I'll have to collect it myself. See ya later."

Bad timing, you think as you watch Peter walk off into the moonlight.

"Chow time!" Tim's voice calls from behind you. He hands you a paper plate with a steak, potato chips and some cole slaw.

"Hold tight," he says. "I'll be right back." Tim returns carrying a blanket. He spreads it out and you sit down to dinner.

"How's the steak?" he asks.

"Perfect," you say. "You're a great cook."

"Not nearly as good a cook as you are a psychologist. I've been feeling so good since we talked the other night." You feel a special closeness to him; he's so gentle and sensitive.

"Do you want to go for a walk?" Tim asks, pulling his slipping jacket back onto your shoulders.

"Sure," you say, shivering a little in the cold air.

Tim puts his arm around your shoulder as you walk slowly down the beach.

"I'm glad you asked me to come," he says softly.

"I'm glad you came," you answer.

Tim pulls you close to him and puts his arms around you. His lips touch yours and suddenly your whole body feels warm.

The End

"I have to finish up here. Why don't I meet you?" you say.

"Rightio," Tony says. "See ya there."

You carefully drop some wool and bits of felt on the table so that when Peter comes in, you won't look as though you're waiting.

"Hello," calls a voice a few minutes later. *I was right,* you think. *Tony was lying.* But when you turn around, you see Carlos, the gate guard.

"Oh, hello," you say.

"I came to see if everything was okay. You were very nervous this morning."

"How nice of you," you say. "Everything is wonderful. I met Tony and Peter and Bobby—and the kids are terrific."

"I knew you would be all right," says Carlos. "Well, I will be going."

"Carlos?" you say. "Do you have any kids?"

"I have a little girl named Maria. She has just come back from Mexico with her mother. She is five years old."

"Maybe someday you can bring her," you say.

"Oh, no," says Carlos. "She cannot come here. Mr. Taylor does not allow it. Listen," he adds, changing the subject, "I have a lumber yard near my house. If you want any scrap wood, I could get it for you."

"That would be great," you say. "We could build barges and sail them in the kiddie pool. The kids would love it!" After Carlos leaves, you wait another fifteen minutes for Peter. He never shows.

* * *

(continued on page 116)

Two days later Carlos arrives with enough scrap wood to build the *Queen Elizabeth*. Boat building is a tremendous success. You invite Carlos to watch the Silverwood Regatta in the kiddie pool.

As he is standing there, you notice that Carlos has big black circles under his eyes.

"You look kind of tired," you say.

"Well," Carlos says, "my wife is very sick and I have been doing everything for her. I don't get very much sleep."

The next day, as you are driving up to the gate, a little girl runs out of the booth.

"Maria," Carlos yells, "get back in here!"

"Is this your daughter?" you ask.

"Yes," Carlos says nervously, "but don't tell anyone that she is here. I had to bring her. My wife went into the hospital last night. Most of my family is in Mexico. I didn't know what else to do with Maria unless I didn't come to work. I need the money."

"She can stay with me for the day," you say.

"No," he says. "I will get fired."

"Oh, you will not. No one will know. I'll take care of her. Come on, Maria. Hop in." Maria gets into your car and you drive to the crafts cabin.

During the next few days, Maria is a regular. She is a cheerful, spunky child and very creative She is even teaching the other kids some Spanish words. Toward the end of the week Carlos tells you that his wife will be out of the hospital in two days.

The next day is the Fourth of July, the busiest

(continued on page 117)

day of the summer. When you drive up in the morning, Carlos is not at the booth. He and Maria are waiting for you at the cabin.

Carlos explains that one of the children has told her parents about Maria and the mother became very upset.

"Mr. Taylor fired me," Carlos says softly. "He told me that I have not the right to bring my child to work. This is a private club."

"But didn't you explain?" you ask.

"He says that I should keep my personal life away from the job. Thanks for taking care of Maria." Carlos takes Maria's hand and starts to walk away.

"I'm so sorry," you say.

When Carlos leaves, you hurl a container of glue across the room. You would love to be throwing it at Mr. Taylor instead. For arts and crafts, you put out some paint and paper and tell the kids to do what they want. You can feel the steam building inside of you. You feel as though you are going to explode.

"Can I do another one?" a little boy asks.

"No," you say. "Arts and crafts is closed now."

At noon, Tony, Peter and Bobby come to get you for lunch.

"What's wrong with you today?" Tony asks. "You look like you're ready to kill someone."

You explain to them what has happened and announce that you are going to quit after lunch. "I can't work at a place that would do something like

(continued on page 118)

that. I never want to have anything to do with Silverwood Country Club again."

"I'll walk out with you," Peter says.

"Me too," says Tony.

"Hey, wait a minute," says Bobby. "It doesn't make sense to walk out without even trying to get a reversal of the decision. Taylor doesn't make the policy of this place. There's a members' executive committee that gives Taylor his orders. Why don't we ask them to meet and discuss this whole thing? I can't imagine that they'll go along with Taylor."

"I can," says Peter. "You seem to forget that this is an 'exclusive' country club. That means they exclude people who don't have the right credentials. Frankly I have serious doubts about the members' inclination to do the honorable thing."

"I agree," says Tony. "The only thing to do is to rally the entire staff to quit. That'll disable the club and they'll have to listen to our demands to rehire Carlos."

If you think that the best way to deal with the problem is to rally the staff, turn to page 77.

If you think you should request a meeting of the board, turn to page 26.

About the Author

JAN GELMAN is eighteen years old and a sophomore at the University of Colorado, Boulder. *Summer in the Sun* is her first book.

Many of the incidents in the book are based upon Jan's personal experiences. She moved from Greenwich Village in New York to Los Angeles when she was twelve, and she spent many hours on the Los Angeles beaches when she was in high school. She played volleyball, flirted with lifeguards and did her share of partying. She also spent three summers working as a crafts counselor at an exclusive L.A. club. And in 1978, her house nearly burned down in a canyon fire. Jan, in school at the time, heard about the fire over the P.A. system. She raced out of the classroom and into the threatened canyon to rescue her dog.

Jan is an amateur photographer, an avid skier, and she is leaning toward psychology as a career choice.